COWBOY DAYS

Stories of the
New Mexico Range

Published by
Zon International Publishing Company
P.O. Box 6459, Santa Fe, New Mexico 87502, U.S.A.
Telephone: 505/ 995-0102

COWBOYS DAYS ISBN 0-939549-67-0

First Edition

Library of Congress Control Number: 2003113978

COWBOY DAYS

Stories of the
New Mexico Range

Stephen Zimmer

Illustrated by Justin Wells

ZON INTERNATIONAL PUBLISHING CO.

SANTA FE · NEW MEXICO

For Shari, my wife, partner, and best friend,
and for my sons, Parker and Marshall,
top hands on the Double Z Bar,
I hope you always have good horses to ride
and good books to read.

CONTENTS

Foreword   6

The First Day   8

A Cowboy's Good Day   18

Uncle Fritz   26

A Day in Cow Camp   38

The 4th of July   46

A Sunday Ride   62

Shorty   72

Amos and Andy   82

Impressing Mary   90

An Afternoon with Tom   98

Donnie   106

Audrey   114

Charley   126

Barc   138

FOREWORD

I have lived in the ranch country of northeastern New Mexico for thirty years. During that time I have spent many pleasant days horseback with friends who punched cows on the ranches of that country.

For the last ten years I have written fiction stories based on my experiences with those cowpunchers. Sometimes I recounted happenings as I observed them, other times I drew separate episodes together and put them into one story. I also wrote a few stories based on legendary ranch men or events of the Cimarron country. My concern was not so much historical accuracy, but to write stories that were true to the range. The result is the collection you hold in your hands.

These stories originally appeared in the pages of *Cowboy Magazine*, published and edited in La Veta, Colorado by Darrell Arnold. It has been an honor to have them in that magazine which is the only periodical devoted to the life of the horseback cowboy. Many thanks to Darrell for his efforts in sharing good cowboy stories with us.

My thanks also to Justin Wells cowboy artist from Amarillo, Texas for the pictures that accompany the stories. Justin is a long time participant and interpreter of range life, and his drawings and paintings are admired by ranchers and cowboys all over the West. He draws the kinds of horses and cowboys that I imagined when I wrote the stories.

Finally, thanks most of all to the cowpunchers with whom I've ridden over the years, sometimes through snow, rain, hail, and wind, but mostly under bright, sunny skies. They are the kind of men that I most admire and hope that my sons will become.

Stephen Zimmer
Cimarron, New Mexico
November, 2003

The man handed him the reins and said,
"This one's yours".

THE FIRST DAY

The alarm broke the early morning calm. Joe turned over and saw that it was five-thirty. A lot earlier than I get up back home, he thought. He slipped back into his blankets, hoping to get more sleep.

He had just gotten settled when he heard the old man's spurs as he walked across the kitchen floor to light a fire in the stove. His dad told him before he left St. Louis to make sure the cowboys didn't have to wait on him, so he sat up and pulled on the blue shirt the cowboy had bought him the day he got to New Mexico.

Joe was at his uncle's ranch because of his dad's worry, not because he wanted to. He'd been sick most of his fourteen years, mothered by nurses in dreary hospitals which only added to his condition. His dad had finally decided he had to do something to help his son.

Disregarding doctors' advice, his father concluded that the only way he could save his son from a life of frailty and dependence was to expose him to fresh air and hard work. That meant a summer at his brother's ranch in New Mexico.

That was why Joe was with an old cowboy named Tom in a cow camp thirty miles from the nearest town. As he dressed, he felt an anxious knot growing in his stomach. The night before Tom had said they were going horseback first thing in the morning.

Tom seemed likeable enough, although he didn't talk much. His skin was weathered and he had a bushy grey mustache and watery blue eyes that were always in a squint. Even though his legs were bowed from years horseback, he seemed remarkably fit.

Joe stuck his feet into the high topped boots the old man had also bought him and then looked over at the spurs that hung on the bed post. They posed a problem. Cowboy shirts and boots were one thing. A lot of people back east wore them. But only cowboys wore spurs, and he wasn't a cowboy. Nevertheless, he figured Tom would ask where they were if he came out without them, so he buckled them on, and walked into the kitchen.

The cowboy looked up from making biscuits when he heard the chink of the boy's spurs. "Morning," he said as he reached for a cup from the white cupboard and poured it full of coffee. He set it in front of Joe and asked, "You want sugar?"

The boy looked in amazement at the steaming black mixture. He'd never been offered anything stronger than milk and prune juice his entire life. But here on his first day at a ranch he was supposed to drink coffee. He shifted uneasily in his chair and shook his head no.

Tom went back to his biscuits so Joe cautiously sniffed the cup. It smelled bitter and, although it burned his lips when he took a sip, it didn't taste too bad. He figured if he could wear spurs, he could drink coffee. Besides, he thought, at least he's not treating me like I'm sick.

When they finished eating, Tom showed Joe where the soap was so he could wash the dishes. It was an uncommon request for Joe because he'd never been asked to do work before. But his dad had said that people at the ranch wouldn't do things for him like his nurses did, so he reached for a plate and started to work. When he was done, he felt a minor sense of satisfaction because the old man only had him wash the plates twice.

After the camp was in order, the two walked to the corrals to saddle their horses. Although Joe had ridden before, the horses had only been bridle path mounts rented for him by his father. He really didn't know what to expect with riding a ranch horse, especially since from the shoot-em-up westerns he'd read he was convinced all such horses bucked. Surely he'll give me one that won't make me fall off the first day, he said to himself.

As he peered through the corral fence at the horses gathered inside, he again felt the knot in his stomach. The twenty or so horses moved restlessly. Tom brought a rope from the saddle room and made a loop as he walked

across the corral toward the horses. They began lining up facing the fence on the far side. Tom drew within fifteen feet of them and with a quick overhead motion threw a loop neatly over the head of a small sorrel. When he pulled the rope tight, the horse turned and walked toward him.

As the cowboy led the horse to the saddle house for the bridle, he told Joe to come inside the corral. When he did, the man handed him the reins and said, "This one's yours. His name's Twister."

The horse seemed gentle, but Joe still felt uneasy. The old man showed him how to comb the horse's back and where to position the blanket. By the way he talked, Joe could tell he was trying to reassure him without letting on that he was.

Tom then brought out a stock saddle which was a lot different from the flat saddles the boy had ridden before. It looked heavy, and he wasn't sure if he could lift it. He remarked as much to Tom who acted as if he didn't hear.

After Tom had the horse cinched, he undid everything and pulled the saddle off. Without looking at the boy, he said, "Now, you do it."

Joe stared at him and thought how silly it was to have to saddle the horse again. But without a word, he took the saddle from the fence and walked slowly with it to the horse's left side. It was lighter than he'd imagined. He swung it onto the horse's back only to miss getting it high enough so that he had to push it over. The horse didn't seem to notice. I'm probably not the first dude this horse has ever met, the boy thought.

When he had the cinch tightened, Tom inspected his work. The man then took the reins and turned the horse in a circle. He stuck his foot in the left stirrup and pulled into the saddle. Joe was amazed with how easily he got on.

The man trotted the horse around the corral a few times and then walked back to where Joe stood. As he stepped off, he handed the boy the left rein and said, "Get on."

Joe drew a breath and took the rein in his left hand like the man had. He reached for the horn and some strings and awkwardly pulled himself on. The horse stood still. When the boy had his feet in the stirrups, he realized he had worked himself up for nothing.

The cowboy noticed the boy's reaction and smiled slightly. "Son, if you could of seen this bronco when he was a four-year-old, you might not be so happy with yourself. We didn't call him Twister for nothing."

The man saddled his own horse, mounted, and led the way out of the corral. He headed for the cottonwood-lined creek that ran south from the camp. The sun was warm on their backs, and the faint smell of the walking horses was pleasant in the morning air. The horses switched flies with their tails and periodically paid attention to Tom's dog, Soli, as she chased magpies.

Then a funny thing happened. The old man started talking. He hasn't said more than three words all morning, and now he's telling me his life story. Being on a horse must loosen him up, Joe remarked to himself.

By the time they got to the river Joe had learned that Tom had worked for his uncle almost thirty years. In fact, aside from a few years of cowboying in Nevada when he was a kid, he'd never worked anywhere else. He told Joe that the Double Z Bar was all he ever needed.

Joe liked the way the cowboy talked to him. Almost like a man. You know, he thought, it might not be so bad staying here after all. And riding this horse isn't so bad either.

Off to the right, they saw a bunch of cattle not far from the river. Tom reined toward them, and, as he did, took the rope from his saddle horn. He pointed to a calf that was standing by himself and remarked to Joe that it had a runny nose. He spurred his horse and after a short chase, roped the calf around the neck. But, as he pulled the slack out of the rope, his horse stepped in a gopher hole which sent them both sprawling.

Joe looked on in astonishment. His mind raced as he tried to think of what he ought to do. He gathered himself enough to ride over to the prostrate man to see if he was hurt. The cowboy was trying to get up but kept falling back to the ground whenever he put weight on his right shoulder. When Joe got off his horse, the man looked up at him with a grimace and said, "Son, you're going to have to catch my horse and doctor that calf. The syringe and penicillin are in my saddlebags."

"Are you kidding?" Joe replied. "I can't do that."

"Damn it, boy, do what I tell you. We can't leave the calf caught, and you might as well doctor him before you let him go."

Joe hesitated a little longer and then helped the man get his jacket off. While he folded and put it under the man's head, the cowboy told him how to fill the syringe. Even though the man was in obvious pain, he patiently told the boy how to hold the calf down so as not to get kicked.

Joe walked to Tom's horse who was holding the calf with the rope tied to the saddle horn. After he filled the syringe, he walked down the rope toward the calf, glad that it wasn't very big.

Holding the syringe in his left hand, he maneuvered himself so he could reach over the calf's back. He grabbed as much skin as he could with both hands, and then lifted and pulled. To his relief, the calf thudded on its side. It kicked and thrashed, but the boy was able to hold it down with his knee on its neck. He injected the medicine into the calf's shoulder.

Before he let the calf up, the boy coaxed Tom's horse closer so that he had enough slack to take the rope off its

16

neck. Pleased with what he'd done, he looked back to see if the cowboy had watched. The man was propped on his good shoulder and returned the boy's anxious look with a painful smile. "You know, you just might be cut out for this kind of work," he said.

Joe caught the man's horse and awkwardly coiled the rope and hung it back on the saddle. He walked over and helped the cowboy to his feet and then onto his horse.

His own horse had grazed off a few yards. When he walked up to him, he patted him on the shoulder before he climbed on.

They rode slowly back to camp. When Joe had the man inside and on his bed, the cowboy said, "Joe, you'll have to ride to headquarters. I'll need a doctor before long.

This time Joe didn't balk. "Okay, I can do that. Just tell me how to get there."

Before he left, he brought the old man a cup of coffee. Smiling, he looked down at him and asked, "You want sugar?"

*He crashed hard onto the ground, and the
fall knocked him out.*

A COWBOY'S GOOD DAY

Joe didn't have a very good day last week. It all started when he couldn't find one of his spurs. He'd taken them off at the cook house when he came in for dinner and put them on the refrigerator like he always did. He was the only one that ever took his spurs off at the cook house. He said his mother never let him wear spurs in the house when he was a kid, and he wasn't about to start.

But after dinner, when he went to put them back on, he could only find one. He watched the crew as they filed out to see if he could discover the perpetrator. He looked especially close at the kid from Nevada. Even though the boy was pretty good help, Joe didn't trust him because he didn't trust anybody that wore short chaps.

He cussed to himself as he looked for the spur. He knew that the kid hid it. If it wasn't him, it was one of the others. One of them was always doing something infantile to him whether tangling the coils of his rope or buckling his cinches wrong.

After about twenty minutes he found the spur beside the cook stove. I'll get 'em back, he muttered as he sat down and buckled on his spurs.

He walked out and decided he'd check on his pet. The ranch mares were in close because they were in foal. He thought he'd take the chance to visit his personal mare, Dolly, and see how she was.

He found her off grazing by herself with her head down. Joe walked up behind her and affectionately slapped her on the butt. She responded by kicking him square in the belly.

She responed by kicking him square in the belly.

20

Joe crumpled to the ground in pain. Well damn, the gentlest horse on the ranch, he thought as he gasped for air. Them boys probably had something to do with this too.

He drug himself to his feet and walked bent over back to the corrals. He sat on the saddle house step when he got there in an attempt to get relief from the pain. Nobody was there as the crew had saddled and gone to prowl the Chicosa.

He was supposed to ride through the heifers. As soon as he felt like he could, he got up and roped out Peanuts from the saddle horses. Peanuts was the gentlest mount in his string, and he knew that with the way his belly felt, he'd better not try to ride one of his broncs. He hurt too much.

Peanuts wasn't a kid horse, just an honest old campaigner. On early mornings in the fall he still pitched some, but Joe thought he ought to do all right for the afternoon. The horse stood business-like when Joe mounted which Joe appreciated because he was in no shape to be athletic.

Joe rode south toward the river and started to feel better. It helped that it was a bright, sunny afternoon without much wind. He thought he'd ride through the heifers as soon as he could and hope he didn't find any problems. He wanted to get back to the bunkhouse and take some pressure off his belly.

When he got to river, he saw a bunch off to the east. Riding closer, he saw one off by herself. She don't look so good, he thought, but probably nothing that a good dose of penicillin won't fix.

He took down his rope, knowing full well that he could just as easy drive her back to the house to doctor her. But that would take more time, and even with the way he felt, it was against his way not to lasso when it was legitimate.

Joe spurred his horse. When the heifer figured what was up, she threw her head up and took off across the pasture. Joe fell in behind her and was about to throw when she ran across a patch of beargrass. Peanuts, being no fool, saw no reason to run through yucca. He stopped hard on his front feet.

Normally, Joe would have kept his saddle, but, as he wasn't working on all cylinders right then, he was thrown into his swells. He crashed hard onto the ground, and the fall knocked him out.

The sun had gone down by the time he woke up. As he came to, the first thing he noticed was meadowlarks singing their last song of the day. It had cooled off when the sun went behind the mountains, and the cold made him shiver even though his face was hot from lying in the sun all afternoon.

Although he figured Peanuts would have gone back to the barn, he looked around for him from where he laid.

22

He couldn't see him anywhere. Damn, ain't I having a good day, he thought.

Joe tried to stand, but the pain in his groin was too great. He dropped back down and started thinking about what to do. Although he wasn't but a mile from the barn, he knew there was little chance that he would be able to walk.

Next, it occurred to him that however he did get back, he'd have to see a doctor. Then he thought how much he hated doctors. They're about as useful as lawyers, he said to himself.

After a bit he turned over to see if he could crawl. He was getting colder and knew he should be on his way. Even if them boys are smart enough to figure I'm gone, they'd never have sense enough to know where to look for me, he thought.

Joe started crawling, grimacing as he did from the pain between his legs. Damn, I wish I would of worn my gloves, he thought as he inched across the rough grass. It had turned dark, and he was having trouble seeing what lay ahead of him. Nevertheless, he was pretty sure he was going in the right direc-tion.

He didn't know how far he'd gone when he was forced to rest. He didn't have the energy to turn over. As he laid there hugging the ground, he couldn't decide which of his pains was worse, that in his groin or his belly which was getting more sore from the crawling.

When he started again, the moon had begun its ascent over the eastern horizon. Good, he thought, at least I'll know where I'm going. Joe looked up and saw a light off in the distance in front of him. Maybe I am going to make it, he thought. As he continued with a brightened spirit, he came to the edge of the draw that ran southeast out of headquarters. He slowly dropped into it as carefully as he could to make sure he didn't roll into it.

But he lost his grip on some rocks as he went over the side and started to tumble down the steep side. Pain racked his body as he rolled into the cold water at the bottom. With great effort, he pulled himself out of the water only to pass out when he got himself to the other side.

This time when he woke, he was in his bed. The Nevada kid was looking at him with a silly grin. Damn, don't he have nothing better to do than to look at me, Joe thought as he took inventory of his pain.

The next day the boys told him how they had found him during the night in the draw with the water from the puddle frozen around his legs. They thought it was funny that even with how dirty, cold and scratched up he was, he was laying face up with a smile on his face.

As they stood around his bed, he thanked them for hauling him in. The Nevada kid smirked and said, "Joe, you sure didn't have much a day." Joe nodded in agreement but couldn't help saying, "Next time, you boys leave my spurs alone."

While we rode, my uncle talked non stop
about some country he wanted to buy.

UNCLE FRITZ

I left the Cross Ts after we shipped in the fall and decided to go see my great uncle Fritz. He was my favorite relation. I'd spent a lot of time with him when I was growing up but hadn't seen him for five years. I wanted to see how he was getting along since my cousin got killed.

I got to his camp at dinner time and found him frying boloney for a sandwich. He was singing to himself while he stood over the frying pan and didn't seem bothered by the market report that droned over the radio. Like I always remembered, he had on a blue shirt with the top button buttoned, button-up Levis, and Paul Bond boots. He also had on the Kelly spurs he had worn for forty years with only a few changes of rowels in between.

As I walked in, a big smile came over his face. Even though he was almost seventy, he still had the same ornery glimmer in his blue eyes that I remembered from when I was a kid.

We shook hands and started talking like we'd seen each other yesterday. Before long, he asked me why I wasn't in college instead of punching cows. I told him I was just doing what he'd done. That caused him to smile. He seemed to remember how he used to tell me that the only honest work for a man was to ride a horse and take care of cows.

After he'd fixed me a sandwich, we sat down and exchanged family news while we ate. The talk soon turned to my cousin who had been dead for three years. Uncle Fritz spoke with his head down and grief darkened his face as he told me how much he missed him. It was the kind of sorrow that a father shows who has lost his only son. His eyes got glassy, and he finally stopped talking. He turned away and looked out the window at the hills to the south. It seemed like he was thinking about the summers we'd all spent together when I was a kid.

I wasn't taking any of this very well and was glad when he got up and started putting things away in the refrigerator. After he was through, he turned to me and said, "If you haven't sold your saddle yet, I could sure use your help putting back some cows that got into the Swensons' yesterday." I mentioned that I thought I could probably find it, and we walked outside.

I started to pull my kack out of my truck when he said I might as well drive down to the saddle house. From that I figured he was counting on me staying a while. I got in, and as I drove by him, I asked him if he wanted to ride.

He said no, that he knew the way, and kept on walking.

I parked by his corrals and walked to the pen by the saddle house. I saw two colts and two older horses standing inside. One of the colts showed that he'd been ridden that morning. As Uncle Fritz opened the gate and walked into the corral, each of the horses put his head up and walked toward him. I could tell that they were in the habit of getting treats.

Sure enough, he pulled some cake out of his Levi jacket and rubbed each one of their heads as he gave them their share. They followed him to the saddle house door and stood when he came out with a bridle. I laughed to myself remembering how in the old days he always roped his saddle horses. Then I thought

He was singing to himself while
he stood over the frying pan.

29

that when you've lasted as long as he has, you were entitled to make pets out of your mounts.

He bridled one of the older horses and said, "Ride this one if you don't think you'll fall off," as he handed me the reins. He saddled the other colt, and we rode west from the camp. I could tell by what he gave me to ride that he was letting me know that he still thought he was more of a cowboy than I was.

We hit a buggy trot for a couple of miles until we came to a gate. I thought that he would expect me to open it, but before I got a chance, he was out of his saddle and had it down so that we could walk through.

We found the cows and put them back. We then rode the fence until we found where they'd gotten out. After we patched the break, we walked our horses back to camp. While we rode, my uncle talked non stop about some country he wanted to buy next to him on the north. I thought to myself why in the hell the old man thought he needed more country at his age, but then remembered that his kind never thought they were going to die.

When we got back to the house, Uncle Fritz started frying round steak and potatoes for supper. Before he started mixing biscuits, he asked me if I wanted some juice. I said okay, although I'd been hoping he was going to offer me a beer.

He opened the cabinet doors underneath the sink and pulled out a Jim Beam bottle that didn't have a label. He

Justin Wells

took a swig and contorted his face as he swallowed. But then he smiled an ornery smile and offered me the half-full bottle.

I held it up to look at what was inside. Strange looking juice, I thought, and weak looking too. I'd seen enough Jim Beam to recognize it, and the contents of this bottle had a strange tint to it. When I smelled it, it smelled liked whiskey, although I could tell there were also some other flavors in it.

I looked at my uncle and asked him what was up. He stood grinning at me and said, "Go ahead and take a drink. It'll make you strong."

Well, I did. It was pretty darn fiery going down, but I decided it wasn't half bad after I swallowed. Of course, that could have been because I hadn't had a drink in three months.

Then I saw what the deal was. He'd gone back under the sink and was bringing up some bottles of liquor in various stages of emptiness. After he lined them up on the cabinet, he started consolidating their contents. He poured what was left of a gin bottle into a jug of Mogen David wine and topped that off by emptying a two-thirds full bottle of peppermint schnapps into it.

As he worked, he spilled some down the side of the jug each time he poured. Each time, he wiped the drips off with his fingers and licked them clean. He shook the jug and held it up. With a satisfied look, he took the

empty gin bottle and, using a small tin funnel, poured the concoction from the wine jug into it.

He said, "Now, let's try this," and took a big drink. His eyes watered when he swallowed, but I could tell he was pleased with the results. With a grin he handed me the bottle.

I already had a warm feeling from the drink from the other bottle, and so I was ready for another. I'd never seen a drink mixed quite like this before, but it tasted sweet and had enough bite to it where you knew you were drinking something.

I was intrigued with his juice mixing procedure, so I asked him about it. He came over and sat with me at the table and explained that whenever anybody came to the ranch to hunt deer in the fall, they always brought a bottle of something. Most the time, the bottles were empty when the hunters left, but whenever they weren't, he stored them under the sink.

Each year he'd build up a pretty good collection. Never being the kind to waste good liquor, he got to where he started pouring like alcohols together so he could throw away the empties and make room for new ones. To make things interesting, he said that sometimes he poured one kind into another just to see what it'd taste like.

He got so involved telling me about his alcohol mixing that he forgot about making biscuits. When he thought about them again, he took another drink and got up to get his flour can.

I took another drink and sat back to watch him work. The alcohol inspired him to more conversation, and he started telling me about how good his last year's colts were.

Then he brought up his favorite story about me, the time he helped me measure some Blucher boots when I was sixteen. The problem was, when they came, my darn feet had grown too big to fit them. As he recounted the story, he giggled about as much as he had when it happened.

Before I knew it, he had the dough rolled out, the biscuits cut, and put in the pan. He'd always been the fastest biscuit maker I'd ever seen. By the time he put the food in front of us, we'd had several more pulls from bottle. I was feeling pretty good and could tell that my uncle was too.

We ate with little conversation, both trying to get as much down as we could as fast as we could. When we were through, I got up to wash the dishes, and my uncle, without saying anything, put the jug back under the sink. He then filled the coffee pot and set it on the stove to boil. With regret, I could tell that the evening's drinking was over.

By the time I finished the dishes, Uncle Fritz had built a fire in the rock fireplace in the next room where he had

Uncle Fritz

his bed. He motioned me to the chair that sat opposite the beat up stuffed chair that he'd been using for thirty years. He'd already pulled his boots off and was sitting in his stocking feet. The fire was warm and before long, the drink and the food had him asleep.

I watched him doze and thought back to the letter I'd gotten from my cousin Ann three years ago that told me that Donny had been killed. He'd been drug by a horse after trying to doctor a yearling bull in the pasture by himself. It had been a senseless death, but one that didn't surprise me. Donny, like his dad, never had patience when it came to getting work done, and they were known to never ask for help if they could keep from it.

Donny had been everyone's favorite, but his dad had taken his death the hardest. They'd worked the ranch together as best friends for twenty years and had taken great pride in the good stock that they raised. Donny's death had so demoralized my uncle that he withdrew from all those who loved him, even my aunt. Rather than share in the grief together, he left her to live by herself at the big house at headquarters, while he moved to the camp on Curtis Creek to suffer alone.

I was glad that even though he hadn't been able to cast off his grief, he still had his sense of humor. It was like he wanted to be sad, but his spirit wouldn't let him. I guess that was why it was hard to feel sorry for him.

Before I unrolled my bed for the night, I decided to spend the winter with him. I might not be much of a hand, but maybe I could substitute as a son.

When I looked over, I discovered
it was a Hereford calf.

A DAY IN COW CAMP

I spent a day at a cow camp once. It was on a ranch at the edge of the mountains in northeastern New Mexico. The camp was populated by five cowboys and twenty-three head of horses and was stocked with a lot of bacon, potatoes, and beans. It was during the fall works, and the crew was gathering cows and calves for shipping. The cowboys were Curtis, Bill, Frosty, Doug, and Dan.

The cow boss had made Curtis the ramrod of the outfit by virtue of his experience and force of character. He'd punched cows for the Bells and Pitchforks and was widely known as a cowboy's cowboy who was an artist with a lariat rope. More importantly, he handled cattle and men well and always seemed to be in the right place at the right time.

Doug and Dan were green but were good horse hands having spent a couple of summers wrangling dudes. Bill and Frosty had partnered for years and had worked on outfits from Arizona to Oregon. They both had a wild look in their eye and had reputations for being outlaws. But no one cared because they were good hands.

The morning I was there, Curtis got up at 3:30 am, built a fire in the cook stove, and put coffee on. Everybody else got up at 4:00 am. I noticed that they all got dressed the same way by first sitting up in their tarps and putting on their hats and shirts. I guess it was a habit they'd developed from sleeping out on the ground during roundups when it was cold.

Each finished dressing by pulling on Levis, socks and boots, and after they stood they tucked in their shirts. Before they walked out to get coffee, they straightened their beds.

By that time Curtis had fried bacon and eggs and was making gravy. When it was ready, he put the skillet on the table and retrieved biscuits from the oven. As I looked at the table, I thought to myself that it looked like he was as good a hand at the cook stove as he was horseback.

After everyone finished eating, they left to catch horses while Doug stayed to wash the dishes. Frosty told me Curtis usually roped out everybody's mount because he was the best at doing it. But because they were only gathering remnants in the Manuelas this morning, they had plenty of time so they let Dan practice his horse catch.

He started off well by catching four out of six with the first loop. Problem was, when he went to catch Doug's circle horse, Gachupin, he missed four times before he finally caught him. Curtis remarked that the horse was about the best he'd ever seen dodging loops.

After everyone got their bridles on and saddles cinched, they stood in a circle while the smokers lit cigarettes. Bill mentioned that his bronc was humpy and looked like he wanted to make war. He added that he just might let him.

When Curtis said it was time to go, Bill pulled his girt tight and drew his horses's head around by the bridle, shortening the left rein. With his right hand, he turned his stirrup and eased into the saddle. The pony stood as if on egg shells. Bill clucked to him, but when the horse didn't move, he nudged him with his spurs.

The horse dropped his head and pitched around the pen. He soon had it out of his system, and Bill easily pulled him up and loped him around the pen.

We had fun watching, but Curtis said we'd wasted enough time and got on his horse. He trotted to the gate

JustinWells
02

and opened it. When everyone had ridden through, he turned and spurred toward the Manuelas. The sun had just started its rise over Saddle Mountain.

It was a pleasant lope across the horse trap. The dew was still on the grass and the smell of ponderosa came fresh over the breeze. The horses started to sweat as they loped along and, periodically, one of them blew wind.

As we neared the pasture gate, Frosty's grey horse, General Lee, decided he felt so good that he started to pitch down the hill. Frosty let him go but pulled him up about twenty feet from the gate. He trotted him the rest of the way and stepped off. As he led him through the gate, he rubbed him on the neck and told him that he was feeling pretty good his own self.

When Frosty was back on his horse, Curtis separated the riders. I was pleased when he told me to ride with him.

We headed north along the fence toward Highland Canyon. Curtis was riding a four-year-old that he called Cracker Jack who he said needed some miles. He said the Highland would be just enough so that he'd know he'd been ridden but not enough to wear him out. It wasn't too long and had a wide floor with several good grassy benches that were easy for cattle to get to. Although there wasn't much water in the creek, Curtis said that he'd never known it to go dry.

We rode to the head of the canyon without seeing anything so Curtis said we ought to split up. He asked me to circle back on the north side and hit the benches as I went. He wanted to take the south because there was a trail on that side that cattle sometimes took to climb out on top. Even if he didn't find anything, he knew of a place where he could look off and see most of the canyon. He told me to keep a lookout for him and try not to get too far ahead.

I nodded and started toward a bench about three hundred yards away. I didn't find anything there and nothing in the next two except for a mother bear and two cubs. She was cinnamon-colored, while her babies were pitch black. They sure were cute as I watched them sitting on each side of their mother staring back at me and my horse.

As I dropped off the last bench, I remembered that I ought to see where Curtis was. I reined to the right and got on a rise where I could look across the canyon.

What I saw puzzled me. Curtis was sitting his horse facing the canyon about ten feet from the edge. As I looked closer, I saw that his horse was set back like he was tied on to something. About that time Curtis noticed that I was looking and waved for me to come.

The way he waved told me that he didn't want me to waste any time, so I dropped down as quick as I could and loped to the place where he'd ridden up. When I was a hundred yards from him, I saw that he sure enough had roped something, although I couldn't tell what it was. I spurred up, and as I approached, he grinned at me and told me he could use a little help. I got down and walked to the edge of the rimrock to see what he'd caught.

Whatever it was wasn't too happy because of the way it struggled at the end of the rope. When I looked over, I discovered it was Hereford calf, who, lucky for him, had a leg stuck through the loop so he wasn't being choked.

I looked back, and Curtis was still grinning. He asked if I could pull the calf up while he backed up his horse. I said probably, and in short order we had the calf safe on top. Before I turned him loose, I asked Curtis what happened.

Curtis usually embellished stories, but this time he reported only that he'd found a cow and calf that he'd had trouble driving. While he was trying to work them out of the pinyons, the calf took off. Without thinking, he'd followed with a built loop and caught the calf at the edge of the canyon. But before he got his horse stopped, the calf went over the side.

When I took the rope off, the calf ran to his mother in an effort to get sympathy over the rough treatment he'd received from the cowboys. Together, Curtis and I didn't have any trouble flushing the pair out of the trees and headed in the right direction. Before we found a place to drop off, we picked up another two pair.

In the distance we saw the other men as they came around a ridge. They were driving eight pairs which Curtis said ought to make the count. When we put our cattle with theirs, Frosty asked what took us so long. Curtis only grinned and said we were just naturally slow.

Back at camp, we turned the cattle in with the big bunch and then rode to the saddle shed to unsaddle. We loitered around awhile while Frosty went to start a fire in the cook stove. He had steak and potatoes frying when we walked in.

Everybody sat at the table and Frosty asked Curtis again what had taken us so long. He said he knew him to be a lot of things but never slow.

So Curtis started to recount his story. His description contained far more detail and humor than what I'd heard, but succeeded admirably in getting a rise from everybody.

After we ate, we all played pitch except for Bill. He sat under a coal oil lamp, immersed in a Louie Lamour book. Several of the guys joked that Bill didn't sleep well unless he read about a shootout before he went to bed.

When we all finally got under our tarps, I thought back about the events of the day and wished that I could visit a cow camp more often.

*Charley was spurring in front and Henry
was seated behind, facing backward and
holding onto the flank strap.*

46

THE 4TH OF JULY

Dave Calahan rode in before noon and found the bookkeeper waiting for him at the saddle house with his check. Tomorrow was the 4th of July rodeo in Cimarron, and Dave looked forward to it with anticipation. Besides, he had not been to town since March.

He unsaddled his horse and went to the bunkhouse to take a bath. After he shaved, he pulled on a blue shirt, his newest pair of Levi's, and the new pair of black Justin boots he had recently ordered from Hamley's. He hunted for his blue and red necktie hanging in the back of the closet and rolled it in his bed. He took his good black hat from the box stored under his bunk and put it on. Taking a quick look in the broken mirror on the wall, he carried his bed out to his beat up roadster.

Dave took his time driving the twenty miles to Cimarron. He thought about everybody he expected to see in town, many of whom he had ridden with over the years. The 4th of July rodeo was the one time in town the cowboys always looked forward to, and few of them wasted any part of it. He added to his anticipation by taking periodic sips from the Jim Beam bottle he had bought the last time he was in town. There was not much gone from the pint because he rarely took a drink when he was not among friends.

When he got to town, he drove to Brooks Mercantile. He wanted to buy a couple of pairs of Levis while he still had money in his pocket. Before he paid for them, he decided to buy a white shirt to wear at the rodeo the next day. He lingered at the front counter before he left, exchanging pleasantries with Zenas Brooks' daughter, Sally. She told him who she had seen in town and made him promise to dance with her the next night.

As Dave walked out of the store, he commented to himself how pretty she was, even though she was looking too hard for a husband. I hope she gets what she wants, I just hope it's more than living at some cow camp, he thought.

After he put his new clothes in his car, he decided it was time to have a beer. He walked down the street to the Ranch Bar. The low slung adobe building had a few cars and pickups parked in front. He looked in the back of the first pickup he came to and saw Shorty Murphy laying in it passed out. Started a little early on his celebratin', he thought.

Dave walked to the truck and shook Shorty's boot. Getting no response, he decided he needed a drink more

than he needed to talk to Shorty and walked into the dark, smoke-filled bar.

He waited inside to let his eyes adjust to the dim interior and then walked to the bar and shook hands with the owner, John Brewer. John always took care of the cowboys, whether loaning them money, getting them sober, or doctoring their faces when they got into fights. The cowboys showed their appreciation by taking most of their fights outside.

As John got Dave a beer, he asked him how branding had gone on the T4s in spite of the rain. Dave replied, "John, you know we never cuss moisture. We brand around it."

While they talked, Dave turned and saw Dirty Joe McLaughlin sitting in the back corner at a table by himself. They had ridden for the A6s a few years earlier, and even though they were now on different ranches, they remained fast friends. Dave was glad to see Joe because he would be the perfect companion to drink beer with for the afternoon. They could leisurely talk cows and horses, hopefully without overdoing anything that might spoil their enthusiasm for tomorrow.

Dave walked over to Joe and saw that he was reading a shoot-em-up western magazine which he always

The two men started comparing what they had been doing for the last six months.

seemed to be doing. Dave thought Joe was looney for reading stories about cowboys who shot guns but never punched cows. The one time Dave had seen Dirty Joe shoot a gun, he had almost shot himself in the foot. But he thought there were worse things Joe could be doing when he wasn't punching cows.

After they shook hands, Dave asked, "Do you work any more or just lay around trying to get somebody to buy you a drink?"

"Both," replied Joe with a smile. Dave sat down and waved to John to bring them some beers. The two men started comparing what they had been doing for the last six months. Joe complained how the boss had sent out his daughter and her husband for two weeks during branding and had assigned Joe to close herd them. He admitted that he really did not mind and remarked that at least he had gotten the boy where he could saddle a horse by himself. From what Dave gathered, Joe suffered more from the nurse maid jokes thrown at him by the outfit than anything else.

They spent the next two hours slowly sipping beer and talking, periodically interrupted by friends who stepped into the bar to get a start on the rodeo weekend. Foremost among them was Henry Marks, the horse breaker for Rand Phillips on the Caliente Ranch in the mountains west of town. Henry was a big man who had a gentle way of making young horses. In spite of his large frame, he was a natural athlete who could sit a pitching horse, whether on the ranch or in a rodeo arena, as well as anyone Dave had ever known.

Joe asked Henry if he was going to ride the next day. Henry mumbled something about how he didn't know if he could afford the entry fee. Dave and Joe looked at each other with knowing smiles. They had heard as much from Henry several times before. In the five years since Henry had been in the country, he had always ridden a bronc on the 4th of July and had never failed to at least show. One time on a bet, he had even ridden a bronc perched on top of an ice cream parlor chair.

Around seven o'clock, Joe took the last drink of his beer and stood up. He looked down at Dave and said, "We better eat."

The remark took Dave by surprise. In the old days they would have just been getting started. Without saying anything, however, he got up and followed Joe out the door. They got in Dave's car and drove the two blocks to Caralina's cafe. The place was crowded, and as they walked to an open table, they stopped to talk to several ranchers who were in town for the rodeo.

They sat down and ordered steaks, pie, and coffee. Once it came, they did not talk much because, like most cowboys, they thought food was for eating and not for talking over.

When they finished, Dave asked Joe what he wanted to do next. He half-hoped Joe would want to go back to the bar. Instead, Joe said they ought to hunt their beds. This time, Dave started to resist, but thought better of it and dutifully followed his partner out of the cafe.

They drove to the rodeo grounds. With the growing dark, there were a lot of cowboys and ranchers gathered with their families. Everyone was either setting up camp or lounging around fires, enjoying the pre-rodeo atmosphere. The two cowboys avoided everyone and found a place to throw their beds in the trees down by the river.

After they were situated, Dave asked Joe if he could use a drink. At first, Joe said he didn't think so, but seeing the look in Dave's eyes, he relented and said, "Well, hell. You know we're not twenty anymore. But I guess it might make us sleep better."

As Dave went to his car to get his bottle, he thought how Dirty Joe might not be as dirty as he used to be. When he handed Joe the whiskey, he asked with a grin, "You want me to build you a fire so you can read some more of them cowboy stories?"

Joe didn't reply and instead took a swig from the bottle. Dave did likewise and sat down on his bed to take his boots off. He took another drink. After he had his pants off, he sat looking at the arena.

"Just for the hell of it, I'm goin' to pay Henry's entry. Then we won't have to go through the motions of talkin' 'im into it."

Joe sat up in his bed and thought for a minute. "Well, moneybags, why don't you just do that."

The next morning at first light, the men put on the prescribed cowboy attire for rodeo day, white shirts and ties. They rolled their beds and threw them in the back seat of the car. When they were squared away, Joe looked at Dave and asked, "Did'ja drink all that bottle last night?"

"No way, man. I got it right here. Figured you might be needin' a bravemaker," Dave replied as he retrieved the bottle, and they both took a drink.

They drove to the cafe, ate ham and eggs, and then went back to the arena. After they parked, they saw Shorty coming around the corner of the bucking chutes.

His eyes were bloodshot and his shirttail was hanging out. When he looked up from under his oversized black hat, they saw that he had a black eye.

"Did ja have a good time last night, cowboy?" Joe asked with a grin.

Shorty shook his head, but managed a smile. "I never even saw who hit me. I just hope he feels as bad as I do."

"He couldn't look any worse," Dave said as he pulled the bottle from his back pocket and offered it to Shorty. The smaller man waved it away and said, "I won't be needin' any of that just yet."

The three men spent the time before the grand entry walking around the arena visiting with friends, many of whom were there to rope calves or ride broncs. Joe slipped away about ten o'clock and went in Dave's car to the Blue Eagle and bought some beer.

When he got back, he asked Dave and Shorty if they were thirsty. Shorty had more or less recovered from his celebration of the night before and said, "I'm not so much thirsty as I'm getting hot." He took the cold beer Joe offered and took a long drink.

Dave looked at him and said, "Take it easy there, little man. You got a long ways to go."

"Don't worry about me, cuate. I might not see this town until next Christmas, and I'm makin' the most of it."

As they drank their beers, Dave saw Henry walking toward them.

"Henry," he called out, "have you entered yet?"

"No, but I was thinkin' about it."

"Sure you were," Dave said as he handed Henry a beer. "Don't worry about a thing. I'll put you in."

He set out at a fast pace for the entry shack and was back in a few minutes with a smile on his face.

"Charley Cochrane's here, and he's, by god, in the bronc ridin'," he said.

Joe looked at Henry and said, "I guess they're just not goin' to be able to give it to you this year, amigo. Looks like you'll have to make a ride before you start spendin' the prize money."

The performance started with some kid horse races and a cow pony race. Henry was not scheduled to ride until the afternoon, so Dave decided to stick by him to ensure that he didn't get distracted before his horse was saddled.

Charley Cochrane was to ride in the morning. He had drawn a big, bushy- maned paint horse that showed a lot of power when Charley marked him out. The horse jumped high, but bucked straight, and Charley covered him easily. The judges scored him 79 points.

Henry was at the fence watching Charley while he rode. Dave noticed that Henry smiled to himself in appreciation of the good ride.

Dave slapped Henry on the back. "What da ya say about that, big guy? He forked him pretty good.

You'll have to ride some to match it."

Henry looked unperturbed. "I imagine you're right. I just hope I draw right."

The rodeo continued with more races, a calf roping and the pack and bed roll race. The spectators and cowboys were attentive to the action in the arena as long as there was not someone they needed to visit with. The sun beat down harshly as it came to high noon but seemed to bother no one. Kids and dogs were everywhere. Most of the youngsters were either chasing each other on foot or riding their pet horses around the grounds, stopping only long enough to retrieve a soda pop or sandwich from their mothers.

After the lunch break, Dave went with Henry to the entry shack to watch him draw his bronc. Although Henry didn't say much, Dave could tell he was pleased when he discovered he'd drawn a sorrel horse called Peanuts. The horse had been to Cimarron several times before, and even though he was pretty trashy, if a man rode him, he usually scored high.

When it was time for Henry's section, Joe and Shorty started to follow Dave to help Henry saddle his horse in the bucking chute. Because Dave could tell that they had wasted little time in their celebrating, he told them Henry would probably do better without their assistance, and that they'd be more help by finding a place on the fence.

Henry's horse was to be the third one out. When it was time, the big man eased himself into the saddle, measured his rein, and pulled down his hat.

Peanuts stood in the chute like a professional. When they opened the gate, he bogged his head and let out a big squall. Early on he made several crooked jumps that would have unseated most riders, but Henry caught up with him each time. Inexplicably, however, half way through the ride the horse shortened his jumps into half-hearted crowhops. Then he stopped altogether, his energy seemingly expended from his early effort.

Henry stepped off and threw the rein over the horse's neck in disgust. Before he got back to where Dave was standing by the fence, the announcer reported his score at 66 points.

The cowboy looked at Dave in disbelief. "Can you believe that? The sombuck quit on me."

"I guess even broncs have bad days," Dave replied in an attempt at consolation as they walked to where Joe and Shorty stood by the fence.

Joe handed them both a beer and told Henry he was sorry about his bad luck. Henry shook it off and said, "Well, so much for that. As far as I know, that horse never quit like that before. I don't mind tellin' ya, it sure surprised me."

Henry looked over and saw Charley standing by the stock pens. He walked up to him and congratulated him on his ride. The two started talking and then walked away out of earshot of the other men.

After the last race of the day, the announcer barked over the microphone that Henry and Charley were going to ride an exhibition, the likes of which had never been seen in this or any other arena.

The three walked quickly to the fence in time to see a big bay horse blow out of chute four with both Henry and Charley in the saddle. Charley was spurring in front and Henry was seated behind, facing backward and holding onto the flank strap. In spite of the weight of the men, the horse bucked hard with long jumps and high kicks.

The bronc's bucking took the men around the arena so everyone got a good look at their stunt. The men hung on the best they could, grinning like they were really doing something. Henry fanned the bronc's rear with his hat before the horse came to a stand still, exhausted from his effort. The men slid off, and Charley casually led the horse back to the chutes amidst the

cheers of the crowd.

Cowboys from all over the arena ran to meet the riders. Congratulations went all around with everyone shaking hands and slapping each other on the back.

Shorty shook hands with Charley and said , "Now, by god, boys, that stunt was worth the price of the show."

The buzz of the crowd continued as they trickled out of the stands. The bronc riders were soon taken away to the Blue Eagle for congratulatory drinks.

Shorty went with them, but Dave and Joe decided to stay behind and enjoy the late afternoon. They got in the car and drove to their camp spot. After they threw out their beds, Joe brought over the box that had held his supply of beer.

"There's only four left, amigo, and they ain't too cold," he reported.

"Well, that's probably all we need," Dave replied.

They sat on their rolled up beds and recounted the events of the afternoon. They agreed as how it had been another great show at Cimarron, and as the sun started to drop behind the mountains, they opened their last beer.

Dave could tell that Joe was starting to fade, but for that matter, so was he.

"I don't know about you, but I've had about enough. You think Sally Brooks'll get mad at me if I don't show up at the dance?"

"Don't worry about it, compadre. You've got a whole year to apologize."

*There was no way you could sit a horse up
against the bank and let a train go by without
it dragging off your horse.*

A Sunday Ride

I was out of a job and riding the grub line. I decided to visit Dick Champion on the Quien Sabes in the Texas Panhandle because I hadn't seen him for awhile, and I thought it might be good to check his count.

I drove to the headquarters about dark. It was before the spring works, so the bunkhouse cowboys had their bed tarps hung outside airing them before going out with the wagon.

Dick came out when I drove up. We shook hands and exchanged a few pleasantries before walking inside. There were four other men camped there, only one of whom I'd known before.

The place was pretty nice for a bunkhouse with a wood stove and built-in bunks. It seemed like it might even be insulated, which I imagine those punchers appreciated especially when northers swept down across the Panhandle.

After I met the other men, we sat around the stove and talked about people we knew and where we'd been. As

*Everybody was watching me like a hawk without
trying to let on that they were doing it.*

usually happens, they were sizing me up as I was them. Even though I was Dick's friend, they wanted to know about me in as indirect a manner as possible. But, by the time we went to our beds, we'd figured we could stand each other.

The next morning after a breakfast of fat meat, biscuits, and eggs, we went to saddle because the wagon boss wanted us to move some bulls. The studying thing started over because everybody was watching me like a hawk without trying to let on that they were doing it. They eyed me when I roped out the sorrel horse from Dick's string that he wanted me to ride. They checked out my kack, my spurs, and leggings attempting to figure out how many miles I'd been. But, I was doing the same thing to them, so it didn't matter. That's what we do.

The day went well. The sun was warm without much wind. The pasture we had to gather was pretty big, and I liked how, even though it was five miles from headquarters, they wanted to get to it horseback instead of taking a trailer. Like one of them said, why not wear out saddle leather instead of the boss's truck.

After we got in that night, being that it was Saturday, we decided to go to Dalhart to see what was there. It was a thirty mile drive, but fortunately Dick had some Jim Beam which helped to pass the time.

We went to a bar which was about what you find all over West Texas and into New Mexico. A lot of neon beer signs and a antique bar on one wall with plenty of bottles behind it. And, there were women there and not all just chippies either. Some of them weren't even ranch girls.

We started out with a few beers, but Dick decided early that since he hadn't been to town for a month and that he was going out with the wagon in a week, we'd better be more serious. He snuck in his bottle, and we put it under a table off by ourselves and commenced to talk about everything important that had happened to us in the last year.

I noticed a funny thing happening while sitting there. Several women kept coming up to Dick, either wanting to hug on him or dance with him. Well, the son-of-a-gun wouldn't have anything to do with 'em. At first, I thought it was just him being polite to me, but then I saw that he really wasn't interested, which surprised me knowing what a hound he'd always been for women.

The night went on, and we talked about a lot of good things, mostly ranches, horses, cowboys, and dogs. I rode the best bucking horse during the meeting, which is how it always happens when there's nobody around to confirm or contradict what's said.

I don't remember when we left or when we got back to the ranch, but I do remember we both thought we were pretty smart before we went to bed. I also remember that we didn't feel very smart when we got up.

Around ten o'clock the next morning, after we'd done the chores and made an attempt to heal up, Dick said we ought to go see his girlfriend who lived over on the LS. I didn't even know he had a girlfriend but figured she might have had something to do with the way he acted the night before. Without much conversation, I just told him I was up.

I started for my truck, but Dick said no, that we were going to ride. He said it was only thirty miles if we went by the railroad, and the ride might make us feel better. I said that'd be fine, being the kind that always liked to see new country horseback.

We went down to the barn and jingled the saddle horses. Dick pointed out a big boned, flea-bitten grey for me they called Grasshopper. He mentioned that the horse was the ranch manager's and might be a little fresh since he hadn't been ridden all winter. But he said he knew how to cover country.

After I roped him, he came up snorting with his eyes real big. Because of what Dick had told me, I didn't think too much about it. The horse stood fine while I saddled him, although he wouldn't stand when I went to step on him. But, I turned him around a few times, and then he stood, and we went out the gate.

Ol' Grasshopper was stout, and although I could tell he wasn't a pitching horse, I knew I didn't like how he took every opportunity to shy at stuff, be it bear grass, rabbits, or his shadow. He just needed riding.

We took out at a lope and by the time we got to the corner of the pasture, Grasshopper looked like he was ready to travel. Dick dismounted and took down the fence so we could hit the railroad right-of-way on the other side. But, the minute we rode through and Dick had tied the fence, Grasshopper started to get nervous. I discovered pronto that he was going to use the railroad track as his next excuse for something to booger at. Although I was getting tired of that action, I told the son-of-a-bitch to go on anyway.

We took off at a buggy trot, when it occurred to me to ask Dick if he'd ever gone along the railroad before. He said sure he had, plenty of times, and that it was sure the best way because there weren't any gates. Then I asked, "Dick, by chance, have you ever come across any trains on these trips of yours?" He replied, "Hell, no, never,"

That satisfied me. After another four or five miles, we turned off because of a bridge that went across the Canadian River. We found a gate and went down to the river. Dick said to let him go first because it might be quicksandy. I thought that'd be good because maybe it'd take something out of my grey horse. But even though we had to swim about thirty yards of sand, it didn't faze the man. The minute we were back on the railroad, he decided to swap ends with me and head north. I didn't even give him the satisfaction of cussing him, although I figured I might have drawn a better mount to take a Sunday ride.

After we lined out again, we went into a big long cut in the breaks where the road went through a hill. It was about a mile long, and I was in the lead. I had my head down because the wind was blowing against us, and I was doing my best to keep my hat on. About half way through, I kind of jumped when I heard Dick cussing. At first, I couldn't hear him clear, but when I looked up, I figured it out quick. There was a coal train coming at us.

Now, there was no way you could sit a horse up against the bank and let a train go by without it dragging you off your horse. Especially if you were riding the nice little kind of bronco I was.

So, we wheeled around and lit out for Dodge. I don't want you to think that I was scared, but I sure put the steel to my pony. And that flea-bitten son-of-gun, well knowing the situation we were in, took to pitching about every third railroad tie, all the while at a high lope.

Now, I'm no bronc rider, but I guess there are times when you're scared enough that you do things that you normally wouldn't do, or couldn't do. I took to riding him like I was Casey Tibbs.

The train was coming on, and the engineer didn't exhibit any apparent desire to slow down. We rode out of the cut right before he caught up with us. I stepped off, thinking for sure that Ol' Grasshopper would throw a fit.

Instead, he just stood there acting like that coal train was no more harmful than a muley milkcow. And what did the engineer do as he whipped past? The son-of-a-gun just waved at us with a big ol' smile like we were some of

his best friends, and he was damn glad to see us. I bet all he was thinking was how he was going to tell his buddies that he almost got to run down some dumb cowboys.

After we checked around and figured we were no worse for wear, we stepped back on. We knew there wouldn't be another train. And sure enough, although my pony hadn't cared about the train, he didn't think it'd be appropriate to let me get back on. Right then, I thought about buying that pony for the killers if I'd lived long enough.

We finally got to the LS that day, and I found out why we went. Dick wanted to announce that he and Janis were going to get married. I told them how proud I was for them, but deep down, I thought we might have gotten the work done some other way. But, like that train engineer, at least we'd have a story to tell.

Shorty stepped out and proceeded to give each one of his pets two biscuits a piece.

SHORTY

I guess about everyone who has lived in cow country has at one time or another made the acquaintance of some old timer who, by force of character, disposition, or appearance, has been especially memorable. I've known several such people myself, but probably no one more notable than Shorty Murray.

Actually, I'd heard about Shorty long before I met him. It seemed everyone around Cimarron, New Mexico had a story about Shorty or at least a description of him. Almost everyone commented about what a good hand he was, a cowboy's cowboy as it were. They all seemed amazed at the immense size of the hats and spurs that he wore despite his small stature. Some said he'd never married, while others claimed that he had, although no one ever remembered seeing his wife. Typical of other cowpunchers, in his youth he was known for taking advantage of his infrequent visits to town. After roundups or at Christmas he was invariably found sharing drinks with friends at the Blue Eagle Saloon or singing cowboy songs on some street corner. Sometimes he did both. Nonetheless, everyone spoke fondly of him and said that his face always carried a smile. He was described as a little man with a big heart possessed of a cowboy's affection for kids and animals of all kinds.

I didn't meet Shorty until about fifteen years ago when I saw him at a CS Ranch branding that I had been invited to. He was in his late seventies at the time and still had a riding job with the ranch. I had just finished dragging the last bunch of calves when I was introduced to him. Being that I had heard so much about him, I took a spot by him while we held herd just to see what he had to say.

We hit it off right from the start, and with only a little prompting, he began to tell me just about his whole

life story. He had grown up in the Cimarron country, although he had left while still young to punch cows in Nevada. Like many before him and since, he'd left because he thought he needed to see some different country and ride some new broncs. Although he didn't quite savvy the long ropes and the "dally welta" that he saw there, he had liked the country and the people he rode with. Still, he eventually got lonesome for the mountains and canyons of his native range and decided to come home, never to leave again.

After almost everything had mothered-up that morning, and we had turned the bunch loose, we rode to the cook house at Crow Creek for dinner. We sat down to the unvarying noon menu served there; roast beef, green chile stew, red chile, fried potatoes, frijoles, and tortillas and continued our visit. I learned that Shorty, whose given name was George, had worked for most of the big outfits around Cimarron, including the Chases, Philmonts, and the Double U Bars. He said he'd always taken camps jobs in the mountains because he liked to work alone and frankly hated it on the flats. At the time, he was taking care of eight hundred CS cows on summer country at the Stubblefield camp located almost to the Colorado line.

That's where I went to see him in July later that year. The camp was situated in a broad valley at an elevation of about 8500 feet which was rimmed by big stands of ponderosa and Douglas fir. There was a good, clear creek running through the horse trap. The camp consisted of a couple of pens fashioned out of peeled fir poles and a solid two room V-notched log cabin made from the same timber. Inside, the cabin had two bunks, a Home Comfort stove, a table, two chairs and a piece of a broken mirror. The only attempt at decoration that I could see was a few old and outdated Frank Hoffman cowboy calendars that hung on the walls.

On one side by the door Shorty kept his saddle along with the few bridles that he used. His leggings hung behind the door. The cabin furnishings were made complete with a metal barrel filled with oats for his horses and a couple of sacks of salt that he packed to his cows.

I arrived in the late afternoon to find that Shorty had already returned from prowling his cows. He greeted me on the porch and told me to unroll my bed on the empty bunk. He then went to mixing up sourdough for biscuits. I watched as he worked and wondered why he was building such a big batch given the fact that he said he didn't expect anybody else for supper. After we ate I found out why.

His horses had come to the back door of the cabin, and Shorty stepped out and proceeded to give each one of his pets two biscuits apiece. He rubbed their foreheads awhile and then sent them on their way to poke around camp and get a drink before they went back to grazing.

After we finished eating and had washed the dishes, we sat on the front porch and thumbed through some magazines and old saddle catalogs that he had laying around. He had taken off his riding boots and slipped into his house shoes. I use the term loosely because his house shoes consisted of last year's pair of Paul Bond's with the tops and heels cut off. But, like he told me, when you've got a pair of boots that fit right, you don't throw them away just because they've got some age.

Early the next morning he called up his horses. Because he couldn't see too well, he had sheep bells strapped on a few of them so he could tell what part of the

*I took a spot by him while we held herd
just to see what he had to say.*

He had sheep bells strapped on a few of them so he could tell what part of the horse trap they were in.

horse trap they were in. All six of them were good, gentle old campaigners who had seen their share of spring and fall works but that were still a long way away from being pensioned out.

After we had caught what we were going to ride, I watched Shorty drag out his saddle. It was a reasonably new Hamley. When I inquired, he said he'd ridden Hamleys all of his life and still ordered them through the mail like he had fifty years ago. He was emphatic when he said he didn't think that there was a better rig made. I remembered how Jiggs Porter at the CS had told me about Shorty's devotion to the Hamley company. He said that as far as he knew everything Shorty had ever owned, including his toothpicks, had come out of the Hamley catalog. Perhaps something of an overstatement, but I had noticed that Shorty had been pictured in several of the old Hamley catalogs that I had seen the night before along with several testimonial letters he'd written stating how much he liked the company's saddles.

After a few days of riding with him, I rolled my bed and didn't see him again until the next winter when I ran into him at the laundromat in Cimarron. He was in the middle of his usual Sunday routine that called for a trip to town for a plate of enchiladas at the Idle Hour Cafe followed by a session of washing clothes. I sat and talked with him about the fall work that had just passed while his clothes were drying. When they were done, he folded them neatly, but then shoved them into a brown paper sack to take them back to the ranch. I noticed that what he washed was simply another set of what he had on, being a pair of button-up Levis, long johns, a Pendleton wool shirt, a black neck rag, a white handkerchief, and a pair of socks. Typical of many bachelor cowboys, he generally wore the same clothes all week, changing into clean ones each Sunday morning.

Since those days, I dropped in on him at the ranch or visited with him in town whenever I could. Not only was it pleasant to pass a few hours with him, but it seemed that at each meeting I always picked some piece of local cowboy history or lore that I found pertinent to the present day. I was his student, and he never even knew it.

Shorty's gone now and, although I guess he never did anything that would make him famous, to me he was one of the heroes of this country. He was just an honest cowpuncher who always took good care of his cows and horses. I'll always remember his smile and what I learned from him, and I'm better for having known him.

*Suddenly, Andy stampeded past him and
jerked the lead rope out of his hand.*

Amos and Andy

On the last Thursday of May, the boss told Lane to get his outfit and some groceries together and pack them to the cow camp in Bonita Canyon. He planned to move the mother cows to the high country on the following Monday, and he wanted Lane to be set up at the camp so he would be ready to take care of them when they got there.

Armed with his instructions, Lane went to the bunkhouse and retrieved his dishes, coffee pot, frying pan, and other cooking equipment from the back room where he'd stored them over the winter. He stuck everything in two canvas sacks and carried them to the saddle house.

Once there he put some oats in a feed bag and hung it on an elk antler by the door. He then walked to the horse trap gate and let in Joe Bird who was waiting for him along with the rest of his saddle horses. The bay horse followed him to the saddle house and waited patiently while Lane buckled a halter around his neck and hung the feed bag on his head.

While the horse was eating, Lane combed him. When he was finished, Lane put the halter on his head, and then picked up his feet and checked his shoes. Satisfied he had a week or two before he'd need to reset them, Lane saddled the horse and went into the saddle house to get his leggings and bridle.

"Now the chore begins," he said to himself as he bridled Joe Bird. He had to ride out into the horse trap and hunt up his pack horses, Amos and Andy. They were half brothers, both by the same stud, but out of different mares. They had been born on the same day seven years ago and had been inseparable from the moment they first came across each other. They always grazed by themselves and rarely associated with other horses in the pasture.

In color, they were both black and each had a star on his forehead. They looked enough alike that the only way Lane could tell them apart at a distance was that Andy had some white in his mane next to the withers. Lane broke them as three-year-olds and had discovered that no matter how much they looked alike, they were as different in nature as any two horses could be.

Andy had been easy. He only pitched a few times and never with much enthusiasm. His brother, on the other hand, was another story. He not only broke in two every chance he got, but he was hard-headed and took three times as long to learn anything as did Andy. He was also lazy and cheated whenever he had a chance.

Because they were such partners and because Amos was the way he was, Lane decided to pack them, knowing he could always saddle Andy if he ever needed.

Lane rode Joe Bird into the horse trap and looked to the far side but couldn't see the horses. He decided to ride the creek where it flowed around a mesa to a place he knew was their favorite haunt.

He found them there, standing side by side, heads to tails, and scratching each other's withers. When they heard him, they cocked their heads and snorted like he

Without asking any questions, they took off in the wrong direction at a high lope.

was a panther from outer space.

Without asking any questions, they took off in the wrong direction at a high lope with Amos in the lead. It took Lane some riding to get around them, but when he did, they turned and trotted to the corrals like they meant to all along.

Lane turned them in at the gate but left them in the outside pen. After they finished the grain he poured for them, he caught Andy and slipped a halter over his head. He led him to the saddle house and as soon as he had him packed, he tied him to the fence where he was out of the way.

Next, he got a rope from the saddle house because he couldn't catch Amos unless he roped him. When he walked in the pen, Amos went to the far corner and put his head up to the fence to make it as difficult as he could for Lane to catch him.

The first loop that Lane threw was right on, but Amos saw it coming and jerked his head away at the last second. Lane smiled and calmly coiled his rope. His next throw settled neatly over the horse's head because Amos misjudged the loop and ducked left when he should have ducked right. Lane thought he looked upset at himself for his mistake, but, with the rope around his neck, he turned and walked toward Lane like a pet dog.

Lane hobbled him and thought about tying up his left hind leg but let the idea go thinking he would surely stand. Things went fine until Lane started to pull the front cinch tight. Amos took the opportunity to aim his left hind foot at Lane's right ear. Fortunately, Lane was watching, and the hoof caught nothing but air.

The situation deteriorated further when Lane hung the first pannier. At the first pressure of the weight Amos dropped to his knees. Undisturbed, Lane hung the other pannier while the horse was still down, and then grabbed the lead rope in his left hand and the horse's tail with his other. Amos scrambled to his feet because he hated to have his tail touched. Lane quickly tightened both cinches and patted the horse on the butt to let him know he didn't hold a grudge.

After Lane tied a diamond hitch over the pack cover, he left Amos on the other side of the corral from Andy and walked to his house to eat an egg sandwich and drink a cup of coffee. Before walking out, he checked his pockets for cigarettes, matches, and Copenhagen knowing he'd probably want them.

Back at the corrals, he found Andy standing fine, whereas Amos had managed to get his left front leg over his lead rope. He'd scraped a good amount of hair off his leg trying to get loose, but at some point had persuaded himself to quit struggling and wait for Lane to get him out of his predicament.

As soon as Lane had Amos untangled, he tied his lead rope to Andy's tail and then hurried to get Joe Bird before Amos could do anything else. Once mounted, he rode west past the hayshed and headed for Saddle Back Ridge which still glowed in the early morning sun. He always enjoyed the view, especially at this time of year when he knew he'd be spending the summer in the high country.

For the first few miles the trail led through groves of scrub oak with a sprinkling of junipers mixed in. It was easy going so Lane nudged Joe Bird into a jog trot until the trail led up the side of the ridge. There the oaks faded to pondersosas, and they smelled sweet as he rode past.

Joe Bird broke a sweat as they climbed the last switchback so Lane pulled up when they topped the ridge. As usual, Andy stood fine, while Amos spent his time wiping his head across Andy's butt in an attempt to rid himself of fictitious flies.

Lane started again before he really wanted but thought it best in order to keep Amos from torturing Andy any longer. It was good policy to keep Amos moving so he had to watch where he was going instead of thinking about how to get in trouble.

The trail followed the ridge to its head and then crossed Fowler Pass before dropping into Bonita Canyon.

Lane thought himself lucky with how well Amos had traveled so far. Only once had he fouled them up by going on one side of a tree when Andy had gone on the other.

About two o'clock Lane and his outfit were in Bonita Canyon and within a mile of the camp. He was whistling and looking at flowers as Joe Bird stepped across a log that had fallen across the trail. Suddenly, Andy stampeded past him and jerked the lead rope out of his hand. The horse was pitching and kicking like no tomorrow, while his buddy behind was doing his best just to keep up.

Lane couldn't believe it. He figured Amos had to be the culprit until he saw some bees buzzing around Andy's tail. He looked back and saw a swarm of them coming from the log that Andy must have bothered when he went across.

Andy stopped about fifty yards down the canyon. His pack had slid to the right side, and he was kicking it with a hind foot. He soon had the hitch loose and the pack cloth off. Having finished that work, he started bucking again and soon had his panniers empty.

Sacks of flour, beans, and potatoes along with cups, plates, forks, and spoons littered the trail for a hundred yards. When Andy quit again, he sheepishly turned and walked toward Lane, while his partner maintained an expression that professed no involvement.

As Lane caught up Andy's lead rope, he stroked his neck. He then looked at Amos and said, "Well, at least he's got an excuse."

As calm as I could, I said, "Mary,
you're standing on a snake".

IMPRESSING MARY

My wife doesn't much care for snakes. I found that out before we got married when I brought Mary to my parent's ranch for the first time. We had only been engaged for a few weeks, and it was the first time that my parents were going to meet her. They were anxious to make a good impression on her and make her feel welcome. Especially my mother.

After Mary and I got there and exchanged a few pleasantries, my mother asked Mary if she would like to freshen up after the trip. Mary said she would, so my mother led her down the hall to the guest bedroom that she had recently repainted in anticipation of Mary' arrival.

The bedroom was in the southwest corner of the house. When Mary walked in in front of my mother, she noticed that both windows were open and a gentle breeze was blowing through the curtains. She commented on how bright and pleasant the room was. Then she spotted the prairie rattler that was coiled up asleep in the middle of the floor.

Mary let out a shriek that my dad and I heard in the living room. We had no idea of what could have happened, so we ran down the hall and got to the room in time to see my mother flailing away at the snake that was trying its best to get away from her. My mother had a hardwood mop handle in her hands and was sure working him over.

She was definitely mad at it for messing up the impression she was trying to make, and my dad and I could tell quick that she didn't want or need any help. After she dispatched the reptile, she draped him over the end of her mop handle and walked out the door, muttering to herself. I understood her enough to say that she would have to find a place to throw it where the dogs couldn't get it.

Throughout all the commotion, Mary held up pretty well. I could tell it had been a shock to her to see the snake, what with her being a city girl and not much used to seeing snakes, much less a rattler in the room she was supposed to sleep in.

But, as I already knew, she was a pretty tough gal, and she was fine by the time my mother got back from throwing out the snake. My mother tried to mother her a little bit, but Mary put her at ease by joking that she thought the snake had been put there specially for her amusement.

Well, things went better after that. Mother fixed a good supper which she followed with homemade ice cream on the porch while we watched the sun go down over the San Carlos Hills. I could tell that Mary liked the ranch and my parents. And it was easy to see that they liked her. They mostly ignored me while they asked her all kinds of questions about school and other things.

The next morning Mary and I took the horse ride that I had promised her months before. I saddled one of my old horses, Centavo, for her, and then put my wood on Flaco, for no other reason than he was the flashiest thing I had. I guess I was trying to impress Mary as much as my mother.

Although this was the first time that we had been horseback together, I could tell right away that she'd been horseback quite a bit. First of all, she didn't need my help to get on, and secondly, she used her right hand to pull herself up into the saddle. I thought that was pretty good, especially since she had once told me that she had grown up riding flat saddles at the stables in the city.

After we were set, we headed west from the headquarters down toward the river. It was a beautiful spring morning, and the sun was shining without hardly any breeze. It was like nature was also doing its best to help us impress Mary.

After we crossed the river, we started up Manuelas Canyon. There was a good trail leading up it toward the low hills on the west part of the ranch. Mary sat her horse easily and kept up a constant chatter about all the different birds and flowers she was seeing.

I had never spent much time paying attention to birds and flowers, but all of a sudden they seemed interesting to me because Mary was talking about them. I turned in my saddle every chance I got to look at her. For one thing, I wanted her to know I was listening, but also because I just liked looking at her. Ol' Centavo was being the gentleman he always was, and she sure looked nice riding him. She had on a blue shirt with her long brown hair tied up in a pony tail. Her blue eyes sparkled as she talked, and I liked the way she used her hands to emphasize a point or show me some flower.

At the head of the canyon, we stopped when we came to the fence. I started to step off to open the wire gate, but

I liked the way she used her hands
to emphasize a point.

Mary stopped me by saying she would get it. I said that'd be fine because I make it a practice to never stop someone else from getting off their horse to open a gate.

I reined my horse out of her way, and she got down and handed me her reins. It was a pretty tight gate, and I could tell she was having a hard time getting it open, even though I was turned around looking down the canyon so that I couldn't see her.

When I turned back around to see how she was doing, I noticed some movement around her left foot where she was standing by the gate post. As I leaned over my saddle horn to look closer, I saw that she was standing on the head of what looked like a baby rattlesnake.

Well, I didn't quite know what to do. I didn't want to start yelling and scare her, but I knew I had to do something so that she wouldn't get bit. I guess before I decided what I should do, a curse word or two unavoidably came out of my mouth. She turned around quickly, thinking that I was making a comment on her inability to get the gate open.

Finally, as calm as I could, I said, "Mary, you're standing on a snake."

She looked up at me, and then down at her left foot. Amazingly, she didn't say anything. Instead, she jumped a good three feet from the gate post and headed lickety split for her horse. I think it was when she was back in her saddle that I heard her say something which I won't repeat.

When I saw that she was all right, I smiled at her and asked her if she was having a good time. She shot back a look that told me she wasn't in the mood for my levity.

I stepped off my horse and started looking around for a stick to kill the snake. In spite of him I still wanted to go through the gate and continue on our ride. Before I could find a suitable weapon, I heard her say, "Get back on your horse. I'm going to kill it, and I'm still going to open that gate."

Well, sure enough, she got off her horse, found a stick, and started beating around the gate post like she wasn't feeling real charitable toward that snake. He wasn't worried because he'd crawled back down his hole, but I bet he was still plenty scared.

When Mary figured it was safe, she stepped to the gate and opened it easily. I think that all of the adrenalin she had running through her gave her the extra she needed to get it open.

As I rode through past her, I couldn't help but tell her that I thought she was really going to like it out West once she got used to it.

Although she tried not to, she just looked up and smiled.

*He liked to saddle another horse and lead
the bronc around in big circles.*

AN AFTERNOON WITH TOM

In the spring of 1988, a friend called and said he was going to go see Tom Blasingame who he used to work with on the JAs in the Texas Panhandle. He asked if I wanted to go along. I didn't hesitate because I'd heard about the oldtimer for years from people who had worked with him, and I had always wanted to meet him. He had become a legend in the cowboy world, what with punching cows for more than sixty years and still holding a riding job in his eighties. There had been articles about him in the *The Quarter Horse Journal, Western Horseman, The Cattleman,* and *Cowboy Magazine.* Ian Tyson had even written a song about him. Tom Blasingame was a hero of our country.

On the day we were to go see him, we drove to his house in Claude, Texas and got there about 10:00 o'clock in the morning. Later, we found out that he usually only spent weekends at this house in town so he could see his wife, whereas during the week he batched by himself at the JAs' Campbell Creek camp in the Palo Duro Canyon.

And unless it was during the ranch's spring or fall works, he especially made sure he was home on weekends during baseball season so he could watch television. Along with cattle and horses, baseball was his passion.

Tom's wife, Eleanor, greeted us at the door and invited us in. She led us back to the den where the old cowboy was sitting in a stuffed chair watching a ball game. He stood and shook hands with us as we walked in. Right away, I noticed the sparkle in his blue eyes and the warm smile that showed from under his trimmed, grey mustache. He wasn't very tall and his legs showed the many years he'd spent horseback. He wore house shoes, but also had on the button-up Levis and red plaid flannel shirt with the top button buttoned that he would have worn on the ranch.

We all sat down, and my partner and Tom started catching up on what they'd been doing since they'd last seen each other. Tom especially wanted to know about one of my friend's private mounts that he'd ridden while at the JAs. He was visibly pleased when he found out the horse, now in his mid-twenties, was still alive, fat, and pensioned out at my friend's place in New Mexico.

We stayed with Tom for most of the afternoon, talking about all kinds of stuff as long as it pertained in cows, horses, cowboys, and sometimes baseball. Being of a historical bent, I couldn't help but ask Tom a bunch of questions about his life and how things had been in the old days. To my good fortune, he wasn't shy about telling what he knew and remembered. He told us some memorable things that day, some of which were so good that I wrote them down the next day so I could remember them. The following is part of what I learned.

Tom said he grew up in the Indian Territory. While in school, he had trouble concentrating on his studies because he was easily distracted when cow herds were driven passed his school house. He said he clearly remembered the sun glancing off the riders' silver spurs as they rode by. As his school career was coming to an end, Tom said farmers started plowing up the country around where he lived and the "smell of that fresh dirt made me sick to my stomach." In February of his eighteenth year, he saddled a big blue horse at daybreak and headed west. He eventually wound up at JA headquarters.

I liked how he described the JA cowboys. He said that they looked like what good cowboys were supposed to look like, big, tall, and wild as coyotes. He said they all had a wild look in their eye. He was even more impressed with the cowboys than he was with the remuda which was the best he remembered of any outfit he ever worked for.

Tom laughed when he told how much harder he thought it was to break horses back then as compared to today. When he was young, the ranches didn't start their broncs until they were four years old, and as a result, most of them pitched the first few saddles. The horsebreakers started each bronc by staking him to a log by a hackamore so that he could "rope burn hisself all over." Then the horse would be ridden for one saddle in a round pen followed by three saddles in a big

pen. Finally he'd be taken outside where a lot of them would first run away and then start pitching. Still, Tom said, most of them learned pretty quick, at least quicker than two-year-olds. The key to it all was that there was a lot of cow work for horses in those days, and they "rode 'em quite regularly."

The first year he was at the JAs, the older punchers took every opportunity to get him to ride their broncs for them, most of which had to be eared down to get them saddled. Tom said that usually when they turned him out with a bronc, someone would throw a slicker or a hat under the horse which nearly always caused the bronc to "chin the moon." The first spring he was at the JAs, he said he sometimes rode as many as eight broncs in one day. After riding so many, he had been confident he would be sent with the cow outfit, but as it turned out, the cow boss wanted to see if he knew how to work before he went with the roundup crew. Therefore, he did get to spend the summer with a wagon, only it was the fence crew's outfit.

The next spring, however, he did go with the cow outfit. After he had punched cows for two years on the JAs, he decided it was time to see some different country and ride some different broncs. He loaded his bed and saddle and went to Arizona. He said he liked Arizona not only because of the country, but of how they did things there. He remarked that the old timers said that Arizona in the 1910s was what Texas was like in the 1890s, "so everybody wore six-shooters and didn't think anything about it."

I asked Tom if he still rode young horses. He said that he did, adding a bronc to his mount every year. He stressed that he did a lot of ground work with them before he ever got on them which involved first tying up their feet then picking them up all around. After he'd saddled them a few times, he liked to saddle another horse and lead the bronc around in big circles with a log tied with a lariat rope to the saddle horn.

He said that his success with gentling young horses depended a lot on good halter breaking at weaning time followed by starting the colts as two year olds. Patience, along with getting their trust, was the most important attribute he felt a modern horsebreaker needed.

Along in the latter part of our visit, Mrs. Blasingame came in with some video cassettes. She said they were copies of movies she had taken horseback during the 1940s of Tom and the JA crew gathering wild cattle out of the Palo Duro Canyon. She wanted to know if we wanted to look at them, which, of course, we did. Fortunately, Tom gave us the go ahead because his baseball game was over.

For the next hour Tom and Mrs. Blasingame gave us a running commentary on the cowboys and horses in

*He had gotten off his horse to rest
and proceeded to pass away.*

the film. It was sure entertaining. We saw some sure enough brush popping and slick roping by those JA cowboys. None of it would have been possible had Mrs. Blasingame not gone out with the crew to get it on film.

After looking at the videos, Tom said that the only roping he did anymore was in the branding pen. Although he said he could still drag calves pretty well, he didn't rope outside much because his arm wasn't "no account anymore."

Reluctantly, around 4:00 o'clock we decided we'd better go so we could get back to New Mexico before it got too late. We shook hands with Tom and Mrs. Blasingame and promised to see them the next time we were in the country.

A year and a half later my father sent me a clipping from the Amarillo paper reporting that Tom Blasingame had died. The article said that on a cold day in late December, 1989, he had been out prowling horseback when he evidently started feeling tired or sick. He had gotten off his horse to rest and proceeded to pass away. The crew at the ranch got worried when his saddled horse turned up without him, went looking for him, and eventually found him where he lay.

I remember thinking what a wonderful way for the great old man to die. He'd been horseback, which was exactly what he wanted to do all of his life. Few people get to cross the Great Divide with so much dignity.

*Judd told him that when he was a kid, all the cowpunchers
rode Navajo blankets under their saddles.*

DONNIE

I always got a big kick out of Donnie. To look at him, you'd think he'd been transported by a time machine. He always wore a white shirt, button-up Levis, suspenders, wire-rimmed glasses, and high-top Paul Bond boots.

He was twenty-seven when I met him, and I found out quick that his goal in life was to dress and do his work like in the old days. His inspiration was Judd Knight, who had been pensioned out by the ranch where we were working. Judd was over eighty, but still active, running errands or doing odd jobs for the cow boss. He even got horseback every once in a while, riding two old campaigners that he'd broke years before.

Judd lived in the headquarters bunkhouse in a room by himself. He'd worked on the ranch since he was sixteen, except for, as he said, the time he'd worked for Mr. Roosevelt in World War II. He was a talkative sort and had an interesting way of telling stories that always assured him of an audience.

His most avid listener was Donnie. Whenever he could, whether at the cookhouse, the bunkhouse, or the bar in town, Donnie would be next to Judd quizzing him about the old days. A lot of times he had to pay for the privilege by playing dominoes, which went okay as long as he payed attention because Judd didn't have patience for people who didn't play as fast as he did.

One thing that Donnie picked up from talking with Judd was the use of Navajo saddle blankets. Judd told him that when he was a kid, all the cowpunchers rode Navajo blankets under their saddles. Consequently, Donnie was bound and determined to get one.

Problem was that when Judd bought them back in the '30s, they cost a dollar and a half, and now they cost more than two hundred. But Donnie was convinced that it'd be the punchiest thing he could do to have one so he went to Taos one day and found a thirty by sixty inch Navajo blanket that set him back two hundred and seventy dollars.

I admit I was proud of his devotion when he brought it into the bunkhouse, especially because he was only making a thousand dollars a month. I made the mistake of asking him if he was going to frame it and put it on the wall. He told me in so many words that he had bought it to use, and that was exactly what he was going to do.

The summer and fall that I worked on the ranch Donnie was camped in the Manuelas Canyon taking care of six hundred mother cows and calves.

Along about the end of August, the boss sent me to camp with him and help him push cows and calves out of the upper end of the canyon so they'd be easy to start down the stock drive when it came time to ship.

Judd drove me to the Manuelas. When we got there, I thought he'd turn around and leave, but he got out of the truck saying he might as well take time to whip the boy in a few games of dominoes. He went into the cabin, while I unloaded my bed, saddle, groceries, and grain. Donny wasn't there but we found a note saying he'd gone prowling and would be back around three.

I nosed around a little, while Judd started a fire to make some coffee. The camp set on the north side of the canyon near where a spring ran out of a side canyon. The cabin was old but well built. It had two rooms made of Douglas fir logs V-notched at the corners. The view of the canyon from the porch was spectacular.

Inside it was hard to find anything very modern, just like what you'd expect from Donnie. In the front room there was a Home Comfort cook stove, a plank table, two benches, and a straight-backed chair. A small table stood by the door with a tin pan and a bucket of spring water on top. There were shelves on the back wall next to the stove that held sacks of beans, coffee, and flour along with bottles of medicine.

Donnie's bed and tarp were layed out neatly on a metal cot in the second room. Aside from some Charley Russell pictures and a few calendars of scantily dressed women tacked to the walls with horseshoe nails, the only other items on the walls were some clothes, reins, latigoes, and cinches hung on pegs.

After I finished the tour of Donnie's camp, I found some saddle catalogs and thumbed through them until we heard a dog bark. Judd and I walked out on the porch and saw Donnie jigging up from his horse trap with his border collie tagging along behind.

He was riding a good looking bay horse and was sitting a new-made, high-cantled, slick fork saddle, the kind popular fifty years ago. I took a double take as I watched him ride up. With his rigging and the way he was dressed, he looked like what I pictured Judd would have looked like when he was young.

When Donnie stepped off at his corrals, he finally noticed us. He waved with a big grin like he was glad to

Whenever he died he wanted Donnie
to have his saddle and spurs.

have somebody in camp to talk to, especially when he saw it was Judd.

We walked down to the saddle house to shake hands. As Donnie pulled off his saddle, I could tell that his blanket hadn't been hanging on wall. He started talking a mile-a-minute, a sure sign of a camp man who only has his dog and horses to talk to.

He said he'd ridden over to the park at the foot of La Grulla Mesa that morning. Then he started quizzing us about things at headquarters, until Judd interrupted him and told him to quit jabbering. He said that he was a busy man and had just enough time to beat him three games.

After Donnie fed his horse and turned him out, we walked to the camp. Donnie got out the dominoes, while Judd poured coffee. I went back to the catalogs and ever once in a while looked up at them playing. I was amazed with how much Donnie looked like a younger version of the man sitting across the table.

At Donnie's urging, Judd stayed for supper. He also agreed to make some of his good baking powder biscuits for us. We all had a good time visiting, and I even sat in on a few games. Fortunately, Judd was in such spirits that he didn't get upset when I took too long to count my points.

I stayed and helped Donnie for a week and then went back to headquarters. He came down a few weeks later so he could haul groceries for the crew that would help him gather his cows.

Unfortunately, I had bad news for him when I saw him because Judd had died in his sleep two nights before. Donnie didn't say much, but I could tell it hurt him pretty bad.

The old cowpuncher was buried the next day on a hill west of headquarters. When the service was over the preacher handed Donnie a piece of paper, and he walked off to the side to read it.

When he was through, I walked over, and he handed it to me. It was a note scrawled in Judd's hand dated six months before. It only said that whenever he died he wanted Donnie to have his saddle and spurs and asked him to take care of his saddle horses.

*From her spot on the porch Audrey
had a good view of the blowup.*

AUDREY

Audrey woke to the clang of the Big Ben alarm at 3:30 am. She pulled on a house dress and brown wool sweater and walked into the kitchen to light a fire in the cook stove. She did not have long to get breakfast because the cowboys would eat at 5:00 so that they could saddle and be at the pasture gate an hour later to start the drive.

After she filled the coffee pot with water and put it on the stove, she sliced enough bacon for Tom and his five cowboys. Next, she mixed biscuits, cut them out, and slid them into the oven to bake.

Ten minutes later she heard Tom walk in the back door. He had jingled the horses and fed them while the men rolled their beds and loaded them into the truck. She saw that he had on the blanket-lined jumper that he wore every fall. She didn't wonder because even though it was only the first week of October, there had been frost every morning for a week.

As Tom stepped into the kitchen, he told her he had broken a quarter of an inch of ice off the horse tank. "I don't doubt some of those broncs will be a little saucy this morning," he added.

He took a cup from his spot at the large kitchen table and walked to the stove to fill it with coffee. After he sat down, he told Audrey that he hoped to get the steers across McAvoy Hill at the head of Cimarron Canyon by noon. He said he would appreciate it if she could bring dinner to them there.

She replied that she saw no reason why she could not. Dinner meant that as soon as she had washed the breakfast dishes, she would start a roast, put beans on to boil and bake two loaves of bread. Cowboys always wanted hot food at noon, especially when trailing cattle.

By the time the bacon was done, the cowboys came in from the bunkhouse. They took off their hats and coats, but kept on their spurs. Audrey went to the ice box and pulled out a bowl stacked with eggs from her laying hens. She started frying eggs after she told the men to help themselves with coffee.

The men ate in silence, watching their table manners as well as they could, especially when Audrey came to sit at the table. When they had finished, they thanked her and headed out of the kitchen to get their hats and coats. Before they got out the door, Audrey brought the pan of left over biscuits and told them to stick a few in their coat pockets.

After they left, she quickly cleared the table and washed the dishes. She wanted to be in time to see the men ride off in case there were any fireworks. She stepped out onto the porch right as Tom rode up on his big grey horse, Chester. He bent down, kissed her, and asked her if there was anything he could do for her before he left. "No, I'll be fine. You be careful," she replied.

Tom spurred into a lope to catch his men who were trotting toward the pasture gate. When he rode past them, Billy Cooper's sorrel horse started pitching down the hill. It was not that the horse meant anything by his bucking, he just felt good. The other horses threw up their heads in mutual interest, but each kept in a straight line toward the gate.

Billy sat the sorrel easily even though the horse pitched pretty hard. He grinned as he pulled him up and settled him into a lope toward the pasture gate.

From her spot on the porch Audrey had a good view of the blowup. She was always entertained when the cowboys' horses pitched, although she was decidedly put out whenever it happened to her.

As the cowboys rode through the gate, Audrey walked back into the house, thinking how different her life was compared to what she had been born to. She had been raised in a wealthy Philadelphia family and had come to New Mexico at age six when her family spent a month at the Bar H Guest Ranch in the mountains outside of Red River. She had come back every summer with them until her freshman year of college.

She liked the ranch and most of the cowboys who wrangled horses there, even though they were much different from the boys she had known back home. Over the years a few had worked up the courage to ask her to go on rides after supper or attend the Saturday night dances.

The only one who really charmed her was Tom McLaughlin, whom she met the summer after she graduated from college. He was thirty years old and had punched cows in New Mexico since leaving his home in Texas. The last few years he had wrangled dudes because the money was better. A lot of people thought it strange he worked for wages even though his parents had a good ranch on the Canadian River in the Panhandle. But like many of his kind, he had wanted to see new country and ride different broncs before turning into a home guard.

The two married a year after they met, and Tom leased a ranch in the mountains at the head of the Moreno Valley. He stocked it with summer steers, and Audrey embarked on a life as a ranch wife. She took to it immediately in spite of living conditions far removed from what she was accustomed.

Back in the kitchen, Audrey stoked the fire and started her dinner preparations. When she had a chance, she went to the bedroom and changed out of her dress into Levis and boots. She pulled Tom's two suits and some shirts from the closet and folded them, along with socks, underwear, handkerchiefs and his good boots, into his traveling duffle bag. Once the cattle were loaded on the train in Cimarron, he would ride with them to Kansas City to see them sold.

When she finished, she checked the food once again and then went out to pull the Ford pickup around to the back door. By eleven o'clock, everything was ready and she loaded the various pots and pans, along with plates, silverware, and cups, into the truck. She would have a two hour drive to Cimarron Canyon if she did not have a flat. Before she left, she drove to the barn, got her saddle, and threw it on top of the beds. She thought she could ride Tom's horse to hold herd while the men ate at noon.

About an hour into the drive down the valley, she caught up with the herd. The cowboys all waved at her as she drove past, not only because they were glad to see

her, but because they knew she carried their dinner in the back of the truck. As she waved back to them, she struck a big rock in the road that bounced the pots and pans. She decided she had better pay attention to her driving so as not to spill their lunch and disappoint them.

When she got to Eagle Nest Lake, she turned east over McAvoy Pass and headed into the Cimarron. The men would follow the same dirt road with the herd before they let the cattle graze in the open meadow at the head of the canyon.

She drove off the road to Tom's usual stopping place. After she got a fire started, she looked in the back of the truck to see if her driving had caused any damage to her meal. To her relief, everything had suffered through, and she carefully carried each pot and pan to the fire.

When she had the coffee on, she sat under a tree to read her most recent issue of *Women's Home Companion*. It was a bright, clear day, although it was starting to get hot. She wondered how well the steers were driving.

About thirty minutes later she looked up to see Donny Chandler loping toward her from the top of the pass. She immediately thought something must have happened with the cattle and got up to walk toward him. When he reached her, he slid from his horse, took off his hat, and excitedly told her that Billy's horse had bucked him off on the other side of the lake.

"He landed on this head and got knocked out. When he came to, his head was spinning so bad Tom didn't think he ought'a ride. He told me to come get you to bring the truck and take 'im back to the bunkhouse. And he told me to watch the food until they got here," Donny said.

As he hobbled his horse, Audrey gave him a few instructions and then got into the truck. She was not too sure about leaving the dinner under Donny's care, but she didn't know what else to do.

She drove back over the pass and on the other side saw the men bringing the cattle through the trees at the foot of the hill. She counted the riders and wondered why only two were missing. As she got closer, she saw that Tom was in the drags leading a saddled horse.

When she was at the bottom of the hill, the herd was about a quarter of a mile north of the road. Tom left his spot and trotted over to her.

"I thought I was supposed to take Billy back to the ranch," she said as he came along side. "Why didn't somebody stay with him?"

"You were until George Moses came through on his way to town and offered to take him," Tom replied.

He stepped off his horse and started to unsaddle Billy's.

"I'm going to need you to help us get these cattle over the pass. If you don't mind, ride my horse, and I'll ride Billy's," he said.

"Well, great day." she replied, "I can't believe I get to go horse-back instead of just cook."

While Tom pulled his saddle from his grey horse and put it on Billy's, Audrey got her saddle and blanket from the truck. She carried them over to Tom, and he handed her Chester's reins so she could saddle.

When they were ready, she led Chester into a low spot so that she could better hit the stirrup. Once mounted, they loped to the herd that was trailing easily over the pass.

On the other side, she rode around the herd and ground-tied Chester about a hundred feet away from the fire. She got the eating utensils out of the truck and had everything ready for the men after they held up the cattle. Two men stayed with the herd, and the others, including Tom, trotted over to eat.

When Tom got down, Audrey took a plate and started to dish up his food. He quickly walked toward her and took it from her.

"Let me do that. You sit down and eat. I'll feed these waddies," he said. She looked up at him with a smile like he had just given her a bouquet of flowers.

"Well, how nice you are," she said as she took the plate and a cup of coffee over to her spot under the tree.

Tom replied, "Besides, honey, you'll need your nourishment because I'd like for you to help us finish the drive. And, oh, by the way, what would you say about going with me to sell these cattle?"

Audrey almost dropped her plate. Of course she would want to go and immediately thought about dinners, dancing, and shopping in nice stores. But she also could not help thinking about chores. Besides, she did not have any clothes. As enticing as the idea was, it just was not part of the plan.

Before she had opportunity to outline why she should not go, Tom raised his hand and said, "I know what you're thinking. The boys can take care of the ranch, and I'll buy you some traveling clothes in town before we ship. And you'n get plenty more when we get to the city."

A smile brightened her face, and she thought, Maybe I'm not going to have to feed chickens everyday for the rest of my life after all.

*He started firing his cannon like
it was the war of 1812.*

CHARLEY

Charley had a way with animals. I'm not talking so much about cows and horses, but wild ones that he came across horseback.

Like the day we rode to Caliente. Charley had signed on for the fall work and had only been with us a few weeks. We were going to camp for a week to gather remnants. We saddled that morning at dawn and hit a buggy trot up Carrizo Canyon leading two pack horses with our beds and grub.

Before we left, Charley strapped on a six-gun. I didn't think much about it being that we were just going to camp. I had no idea if he could hit anything with it and only figured he had it along in case he saw a coyote.

We were making good time when a cottontail jumped out from behind a pinon tree. Charley pulled up his horse and got down. Before I could do the same, he started firing his cannon like it was the War of 1812.

My horse had never heard a gun go off, and he showed me real quick he didn't like anything about it. He swapped ends and started to sell out, but I got him stopped before he could bog his head. I turned him around and rode back to where Charley was reloading his gun.

Charley was mumbling to himself about how he had almost hit the rabbit twice and that, by god, he was going to hit him this time because we were going to have rabbit for supper. I didn't think it was worth telling him that we had a side of beef hanging in camp, so I got off my horse and started looking to see if I could see the rabbit.

The rabbit hadn't gone too far, I guess because he was scared out of his wits. He was trying to hide under a little bush, shaking like all get out. I picked up a couple of rocks and threw one at him to get him going. When he broke from his cover, I sailed another one and hit him square in the head.

After I did it, I felt bad. Without admitting to Charley that most of the time I couldn't hit a barn with a rock, I walked over and picked up the rabbit. I strolled back to Charley and nonchalantly said, "The next time you need camp meat, just ask me."

Charley looked down at his gun that he still hadn't got loaded and shook his head. I tied the rabbit by a string behind his saddle, and, without looking at him, got on my horse and headed to camp.

It was almost dark when we got there, so I told Charley to grain the horses and turn them into the trap. I went inside and built a fire in the stove. Before long, I

was frying beefsteak and had biscuits ready for the oven.

Charley walked in and pulled
off his chaps. He didn't say much as
he unrolled his bed onto one of the
empty bunks. After he was squared
away, he sat on his bed acting like
he was thinking. He pulled his gun
out, spun the cylinder a few times,
and then shoved it back into the
holster. He got up, unbuck-
led the belt, and carefully put
it in his war bag. I never saw
him wear it again as long as he was
on the ranch.

The next morning when we woke up, I
couldn't help but notice how many shirts he
put on. It was only early October and not very
cold yet, but he dressed like we were camped in
the Klondike. He started cowboy fashion by
sitting up in bed and pulling on a T-shirt. Then
he put on another one. And then
another one.

*I never saw him wear it again as
long as he was on the ranch.*

129

Next he pulled on a regular shirt, and then put a wool shirt over that. How in the world he was able to tuck all those shirts in, I'll never know. I guess when he got to the high country, he took a chill because the day before he only wore one shirt and a Levi jacket. I wondered if maybe he'd never punched cows in the mountains before and thought he'd have to wear plenty of garments during the fall works so he wouldn't catch cold. Seemed peculiar to me.

We spent an uneventful week in camp and found all of our cattle. Although he was pretty young, he proved to be a lot of help. He always seemed to be where he should be and was a darn good tracker. His talent that way made our work go a lot quicker.

Aside from all the shirts he put on, he seemed regular enough. He rode a fairly new Hamley saddle with a Daisy Mae stamp and had several nice silver mounted bits stashed in his war bag. By the looks of his outfit, you could tell that he liked to take care of his equipment. I figured he never spent much of his wages on anything else except beer when he went to town.

On the day we rode home another unusual thing happened to him. We were trotting in at a good clip and were probably not more than a mile from the house. Charley was ahead of me when he suddenly pulled up his horse. He got down quick, picked up a big stick, and started beating around the bush he'd just ridden past.

When I got to him, he was yelling that a snake had just bit his horse. Sure enough, as I looked closer there was a rattler inside the bush doing his best to get away from Charley. It had been warm enough down at headquarters that we were still seeing some snakes, and this one had sure got his horse. All I could think was that something had stirred him up so much right before Charley rode by that he'd struck the first thing that passed his way. That happened to be Charley's horse.

Charley finally got him killed. I thought, Just this cowboy's luck. But I couldn't help saying to him that I bet he wished he hadn't put away his six gun.

We rode on to the corrals. After Charley got his horse unsaddled, he washed the snake bite. Because the snake probably didn't have much poison when he bit the horse, the leg never did swell.

Charley

A few days later Charley and I were riding through the Saloon pasture looking for cattle. The pasture was in the foothills and had a lot of juniper, pinon, and oak brush in it. Along about mid morning, we were separated by about half a mile when I heard Charley yelling for me from over in a brushy side canyon. I immediately thought, What in the hell has he got into now?

I hit a lope to where I had heard him. He was off his horse, and as I rode up, he had his pocket knife out and was leaning over two buck deer. They were layed out flat with their heads facing each other. The ground all around them was torn up like they'd been fighting.

He turned and looked at me and said, "Would ya look at this?"

In the process of their fight the bucks had gotten their antlers locked together. They weren't moving as far as I could see, and I thought both of them were dead.

But then Charley said, "One of 'em's still breathin'."

Sure enough, when I walked over, I could see that one of them was panting heavily. Sweat covered his body. The other one's eyes were glazed over to where it looked like he'd been dead for a while.

We both looked at each other and finally Charley asked, "What do you think we should do?"

"Well, I guess we oughta put the poor guy out of his misery." Charley slowly shook his head, and looked around the ground and then up in the sky. He finally said,

"No, I'm going to try to save him."

He went to work trying to unhook their antlers. I stood there watching him a minute thinking the deer would probably never get up even if he got them separated. But seeing how hard Charley was trying to help him, I walked over to see what I could do.

The bucks were sure locked tight. From the looks of things, they had spent most their time just trying to get away from each other after they'd got hooked. The dead one had finally tuckered from the battle because it didn't look like he had any serious wounds otherwise.

Try as we might, the dead weight of the bucks was so much that we couldn't get their antlers apart. Finally, Charley picked up his pocket knife that he had dropped and started cutting around the dead one's neck. I took out my knife and did the same. Soon we were down to the bone and with quite a bit more effort we were able to break the deer's neck so that we could just work with his head.

We'd gotten tired with our labor so we sat cross-legged on the ground and took a breather. We started talking about what to do next. Looking at the locked heads, it seemed that the buck that was still alive was doing all right, although he was pretty scared. He hadn't moved much probably because he didn't have the energy to do anything.

Suddenly, I remembered something I had in my saddle pockets. Without saying anything to Charley, I got up

and walked to my horse. I rummaged around in the near side pocket and found what I was looking for. A Swiss Army knife. One of those ones with a million attachments. I'd always been kind of embarrassed packing it around knowing that it wasn't very punchy, but I'd been amazed over the years how many times I'd found use for it when I was out horseback.

I walked back over to Charley. He looked at me funny as I started pulling out the blades looking for the one I wanted. Finally, I came across the right one. A saw.

I said to Charley, "Maybe if we cut off the points where they're really hooked, we could get 'em apart. At least it's worth a try, unless you've got a better idea."

Charley looked at me like I was still crazy, but turned back to the deer and said, "Well, let's just see what your little red knife will do."

I leaned over the deer and started sawing where I thought it would do the most good. As I was doing it, I couldn't help thinking about how many cattle we had to gather, but kept right on until we finally got the dead deer's head away from the one that was alive.

We stepped back, and I rubbed my fingers that were sore from sawing with the knife. After a short time, the buck realized that he could move his head. He had gathered enough strength laying there to where he thought he could try to get up. After a few tries he got to his feet.

He wobbled there a minute and slowly got himself oriented. Before he walked off, he looked over at us, shook his head, and snorted.

Charley turned my way and said, "Is that all the thanks we get?"

I said, "I don't know, but I bet he's glad you didn't have your six shooter on you."

*Neither one of us hankered to spend
a winter in Montana to find out.*

BARC

After Christmas, the boss told Barc and me that he wanted us to break ice for the next month. That suited us fine because we wouldn't have to feed. It didn't take two men to break ice, but the boss thought it'd be better if there were always two of us along. We didn't argue, because we'd have somebody to talk to, and we liked the idea of being horseback every day even though it would be during the coldest month of the year.

Barc had only been with us since last spring, coming out of the Texas Panhandle. He'd turned out to be a good hand and always seemed to be in the right place. I liked working with him.

The day I remember most about that month came during the second week of January. That morning I saddled a bronc I called Ramrod that I had started the summer before. He was a stout four-year-old that was coming along pretty well, although he still liked to find boogers where ever he could find them. He was steady enough for his age, but like all of his kind he needed a lot of riding.

Barc also decided to ride one of his broncs, a compact little sorrel that he called Dot because of a white spot on his forehead. We left headquarters about 7:00 o'clock each equipped with a three-quarter axe tied on the off side of our saddles.

We had eight spots to check, either dirt tanks or creeks, that we broke open for the cattle or turned out saddle horses. The circle was about fifteen miles long, and if we got an early enough start, we were usually back in time to unsaddle before dinner.

It hadn't snowed for a few days and the foot of snow that we rode through had a hard crust on it. Breath plumes rolled out of our horses' noses as we headed north out of the corrals at a good trot.

The rising sun on our right seemed warm even though it was below freezing. As usual, it didn't seem all that cold because it was clear and dry and the wind hadn't come up. We both wore blanket-lined jumpers in addition to the long johns that we hadn't been without for the last two months.

When we came to the outside gate of the horse trap, Barc loped ahead to open it. After he closed it and stepped back on, we hit a lope toward the tank that was in the middle of the Martinez. We always took turns breaking ice, and so since Barc had already opened a gate, I untied my axe and got down.

The ice was only about two inches thick where we'd been cutting it out for the last few weeks. We always

140

broke out as big of pieces of ice as we could so they could be fished out to keep the hole clear as long as possible.

As I was chopping, Barc asked me what I thought it was probably like up in Montana and the northern ranges in the winter. After some discussion, we decided that even though it got pretty cold down here in the high country of New Mexico, it couldn't be anywhere like it must be up there. Neither one of us hankered to spend a winter in Montana to find out.

After I got back on, we headed west toward Manuelas Canyon. There were two hundred first calf heifers in there, and besides breaking ice for them in the creek, we'd have a chance to ride through them to see if anything might already be springing.

As we rode up the creek to where we usually broke ice, we noticed up ahead some ravens and magpies flying around a spot on the other side. I told Barc to go ahead and cut the ice, and I would cross over and investigate the birds. Hopefully, they were just eating on a dead deer or elk and not one of our heifers.

I picked a spot on the creek above where Barc was going to work. As I pointed Ramrod across the ice, it seemed that it was plenty thick and that he shouldn't have trouble walking on it. He balked a little bit as I pointed him in and shuffled his feet, but finally he started across. The creek wasn't more than twenty feet across where we were and looked like it was rocky all the way.

Ramrod kept his nose down as he slowly moved over the ice. There were some willows on the far side where the main part of the current ran, and he hesitated as he got nearer to them.

I got impatient and jobbed him with both spurs to persuade him to get across. Being a colt, he lunged more than he needed to but still didn't make the bank. Instead, he broke through the ice, and suddenly I found Ol' Ramrod had jumped us in the middle of a hole that I hadn't seen, but that evidently he had. It probably wasn't more than two feet deep, but deep and slippery enough to where it was hard for him to climb out.

He started thrashing around with no more result than getting us both wet. I tried to settle him, but before I could, he lost his feet.

He fell on his right side, and before I could kick out, he pinned my leg underneath him. Cold water flooded over my back. I tried to reach his bridle because I'd lost my reins, but he had me in a position where I couldn't grab it.

As I started thinking about what I ought to do, I realized that Barc had gotten off of his horse, crossed the creek, and grabbed my horse by the head.

He was kneeling half on the ice and half in the water. I knew without him telling me that he was going to keep the horse's head down long enough so that he wouldn't run off with my foot in the stirrup.

When Barc thought it was time, he stepped back. Ramrod scrambled to his feet, and Barc got him by the reins. Sure enough, my spur was caught in the back cinch, but the horse didn't move. Instead, he stood shaking, scared, but maintaining himself.

I was able to grab the back cinch so that I could pull myself up and get my foot out of the stirrup. I got to my feet as soon as I could, shaking pretty good my ownself.

Being a colt, he lunged more than he needed to.

When I looked at Barc, he grinned and asked me if there wasn't somewhere else I could take a bath. Although I tried not to, I smiled back and told him he might as well take one seeing as how he'd already got a start.

Since we were only five miles from the house, we decided to lope back, warm up and change clothes. As I stepped on ol' Ramrod, I told him how proud I was of him. And then I told Barc the very same thing.